HOW to BEAT THE BULLY

Without Really Trying

SCOTT STARKEY

HOW to BEAT THE BULLY Without Really Trying

A PAULA WISEMAN BOOK
Simon & Schuster Books for Young Readers
New York London Toronto Sydney New Delhi

SIMON & SCHUSTER BOOKS FOR YOUNG READERS
An imprint of Simon & Schuster Children's Publishing Division
1230 Avenue of the Americas, New York, New York 10020

For information about special discounts for bulk purchases, please contact Simon & Schuster Special Sales at 1-866-506-1949 or business@simonandschuster.com.
The Simon & Schuster Speakers Bureau can bring authors to your live event. For more information or to book an event, contact the Simon & Schuster Speakers Bureau at 1-866-248-3049 or visit our website at www.simonspeakers.com.
Also available in a Simon & Schuster Books for Young Readers hardcover edition.
Book design by Krista Vossen
The text for this book is set in Bembo Std.
Manufactured in the United States of America • 1112 OFF
First Simon & Schuster Books for Young Readers paperback edition January 2013
The Library of Congress has cataloged the hardcover edition as follows:
Starkey, Scott.
How to beat the bully without really trying / Scott Starkey.
p. cm.
"A Paula Wiseman Book."
Summary: Rodney, an admitted coward, moves to Ohio where the middle-school bully immediately singles him out, but when a stray baseball knocks the bully out just as he is about to beat Rodney up, Rodney gains an undeserved reputation as a tough guy.
ISBN 978-1-4424-1685-7 (hc)
[1. Bullies—Fiction. 2. Schools—Fiction. 3. Ohio—Fiction. 4. Humorous stories.]
I. Title.
PZ7.S7952Ho 2012
[Fic]—dc23
2011019439
ISBN 978-1-4424-8473-3 (pbk)
ISBN 978-1-4424-1693-2 (eBook)

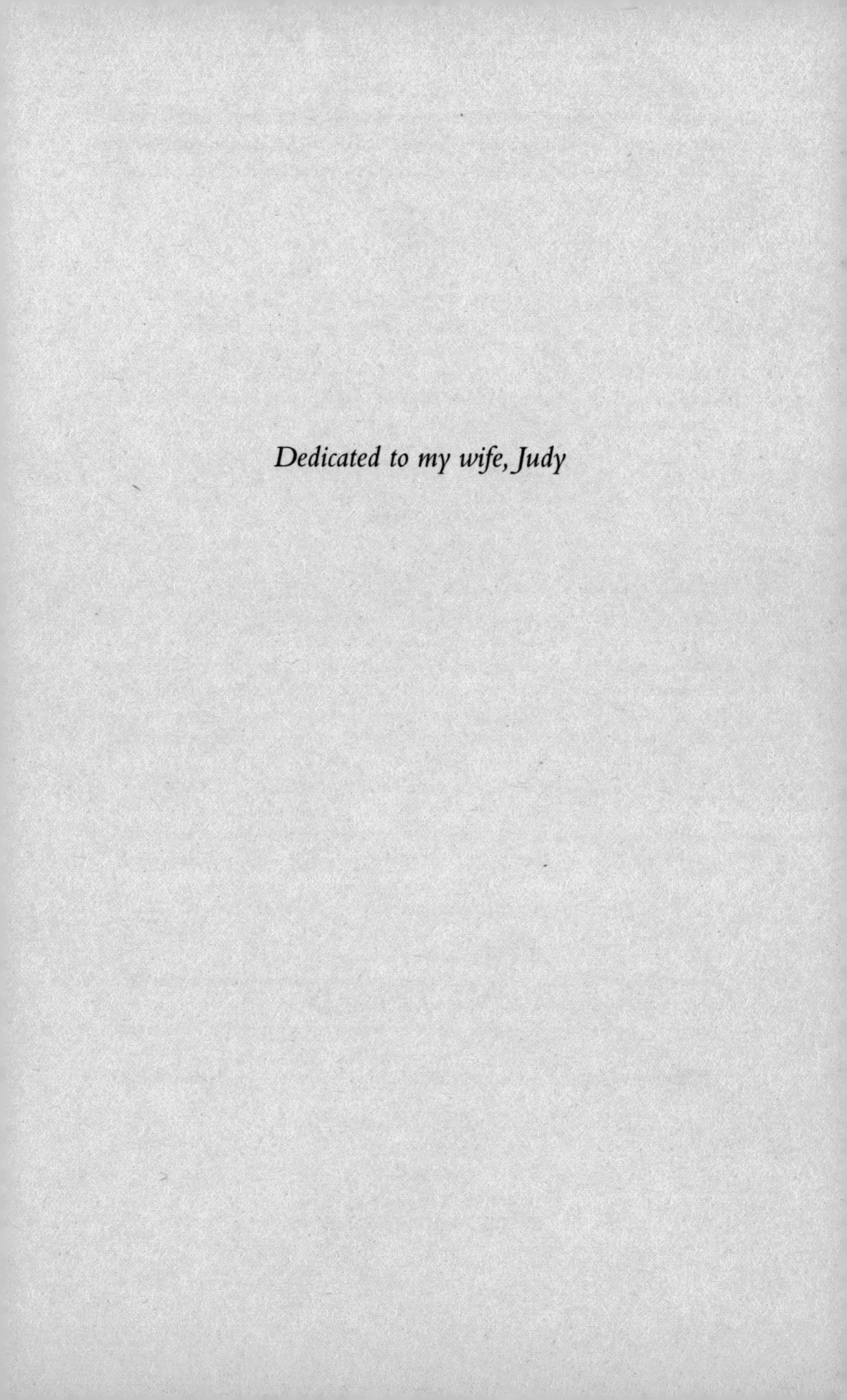

Dedicated to my wife, Judy

Acknowledgments

In writing this book, there were many people who helped me along the way. I will always appreciate the help and interest given to me by Jim Trelease. I am also grateful to my agent, Barbara Kouts, and my editor, Paula Wiseman, for this wonderful opportunity and their guidance. I owe much of my inspiration to my past and present students in room 303 at East Street Elementary.

And above all, I thank my great friend Lloyd Singer. Without his edits, ideas, and encouragement, this book would have never become a reality.

CONTENTS

HOW to BEAT THE BULLY

Without Really Trying

Chapter 1

NOWHERE TO HIDE

"So what'll it be, a black eye or a bloody nose?"

"What's the third choice?" I asked.

He looked confused. "Enough talking. Ready to die, new kid?"

Ah, the first day of school! New notebooks, a new backpack, meeting new people, getting beat up by a bully. Actually, Josh wasn't just any bully. He was THE bully at Baber Intermediate. Looking back on it now, I can't believe I made it through that first day. Heck, I can't believe I survived all the way to graduation. It's a pretty amazing story to tell. Adults will probably say I'm exaggerating, but I don't blame them. Even I have a hard time believing what happened to me this year!

I remember exactly how I felt that first morning before school. My father was sitting to my left at the breakfast table. He was in the middle of buttering some toast when he turned to me and asked, "Rodney, what could be better than being a new kid in a new school in a new state? This must be your lucky day!" It's hard to imagine, but he really believed the nonsense that came out of his mouth. He sat there at the breakfast table grinning from ear to ear. "Can't you just *feel* the excitement?"

All *I* could feel was my stomach twisting into a tight knot. Today was going to be the worst day ever—and I didn't even know yet about Josh, the lunchtime fight, the broken nose, and everything else waiting for me at school.

My little sister, Penny, shouted, "Rodney's turning green!"

Panic flashed across my dad's face. "I can't be late for work." He jumped up and was out the door like a shot.

My mom watched him leave and shook her head slightly. "He'll never get over the shoe incident." Listening, I remembered how he'd been smiling when he told me we were moving to Ohio. I also remembered how the smile had faded when I'd thrown up on his foot.

"Anyway, Rodney," my mother continued, "don't worry about today. Everyone's going to love you. Isn't that right, Penny?"

"Sure, just like in New York," she answered, never missing an opportunity to torture her older brother.

I looked down at my bowl of Cheerios, remembering some of the bullies I had left behind. But as bad as they were, the idea of being the new kid scared me even more. You see, I knew what my parents didn't—that I'm a coward. Not just your average wimp, afraid of the occasional creepy movie or dark basement steps, but the real deal, a big-time chicken. I'd rather run than fight anytime. Penny was the only one in my family who guessed the truth about me.

My mom handed me my lunch and I headed out the door for the bus stop. As I approached the end of our street, I realized I didn't know any safe hiding spots. In my old school I knew where to hide when a bully came looking for me. Luckily, there were no menacing thugs about—just one kid at the bus stop leaning against a big maple tree and fidgeting with something in his hands. He wasn't much taller than me, which isn't saying much. He had black hair and a warm face that broke into a grin when he saw me approach.

"Hey, you're that new kid. What's your name?"

"I'm Rodney." This was going well.

"Rodney? They're going to kill you with a name like that."

I felt my stomach tighten. "What's *your* name?" I asked.

"Rishi."

For a moment I just stared at him, not knowing what to say. "Rishi?" I repeated.

"Where you from?" he asked.

"New York," I told him.

"New York. Wow . . . do you ride the subway every

day? How many times have you been mugged?"

He'd seen too many movies. Nothing dangerous ever happened in my old neighborhood, which was in the outskirts of New York City in Queens. I tried to think of something to say.

"Oh, I get it," he kept talking. "Can't speak about it, right? Don't want to be a rat, huh? Okay, who's your teacher? Can you answer that?"

"Mrs. Lutz-something," I started to say, wondering if this Rishi kid ever stopped blabbering.

"Wow, me too. Hey look, there's the bus. Stick with me. I'll show you around the place. Smile." Click!

"What the . . . ?" I started to ask.

"No worries, I take pictures of everything." Rishi kept right on talking as we climbed aboard the bus. He pointed to a seat in the middle and sat down next to me. He never shut up, but he was nice. I relaxed a little. I had already made a friend. Maybe things wouldn't be so bad. It was then that I noticed he *had* shut up. "Keep your head down," he whispered.

"Huh? What? Why . . ."

"Shhhhh. This is Josh's bus stop."

The rest of the bus had gone silent. "Who's Josh?"

Rishi looked at me like I was crazy. "Only the nastiest bully in Baber Intermediate history. He was beating up kids our size back in nursery school. Keep your head down. Don't look him in the eye and maybe you'll be all right. See you later."

"What? Where are you going?"

"Oh, he *hates* new kids. Good luck." With that, he ducked a few seats away, leaving me in terror. *Oh no no no-o-o-o-o,* my brain seemed to scream. I noticed the girl across the aisle hiding behind her backpack, and I considered climbing under the seat. The doors opened and loud footsteps thudded up the stairs. In the end I just closed my eyes and tried to imagine something happy. The only thing that came to mind was my sister's favorite TV show growing up. I sat there quietly humming, "I love you, you love me, we're a happy family," and waited for the end to come.

The steps got closer and a bead of sweat ran down my spine. After what seemed a very long time, the bus started. I couldn't believe it. He had left me alone! That wasn't so bad. I exhaled and started to open my . . .

Smack!

My head jerked forward and stung in the back. I looked up to see a kid staring down at me. He looked six feet tall and had a neck the size of my waist. "You a new kid?" he growled.

For a second I considered jumping out the emergency hatch, but then managed to squeak, "Me? No, I'm not *new*. Been here for years."

"How come I ain't seen you?"

"Uh, well, I'm very forgettable. My mom sometimes forgets my name and . . ."

"You lyin' to me, kid? 'Cause if you *are* . . ."

"What? Me? No. I'd never lie."

"You'd better not be. I'll be seeing you real soon."

"Oh, okay, look forward to it," I said. He grunted and gave my head another smack before strutting down the aisle to the back of the bus. I exhaled. *Yeah, Mom. They're all going to love me.*

Eventually the bus pulled up in front of Baber Intermediate. It was a pretty typical-looking school, not old but not brand-new. All I kept thinking was how much space there was out here in the Midwest. Fields and fields everywhere. Back in New York we all lived on top of each other.

I went through the main entrance and was heading down a crowded corridor, careful to avoid Josh, when Rishi appeared at my elbow. "You're still alive?" he observed.

Barely, I thought.

"You probably don't know where Mrs. Lutzkraut's class is. Come with me." We climbed a set of stairs, went down another long hall, and came to a stop outside room 217. "Now look, Mrs. Lutzkraut is mean," Rishi explained.

Just wonderful. My brain sighed.

"Some of my good buddies are in this class, though. Real good guys. Let's go meet them."

It sounded like an excellent idea. I felt a little relief, especially since Josh was nowhere in sight. Time to finally meet some nice kids. I walked up to the first boy in line and said, "Hi, I'm Rodney."

He looked at me through narrow eyes. "Rodneeeeey. Nice name. So, you new here?"

I smiled. "Yes, I am."

"That's just great, 'cause me and my buddy Josh love getting to know the new kids." He cracked his knuckles and turned away from me. That wasn't good.

Realizing I'd just totally blown it, I crept back to Rishi. "I thought you said your buddies were nice?"

"My buddies *are* nice. He's not my buddy. That was Toby. You should have stayed far away from him."

"How was I . . ."

"Who is talking in this hall?" snapped a sharp grown-up voice. Rishi bowed his head and slid into line. I looked up to see who had yelled.

It was an awful sight, so bad I almost didn't hear her shout, "I will *not* have such behavior in my class, do you *hear*?" For starters, this lady looking down at me was old. Her hair was short and curly and colored some strange, unnatural orange. Her glasses were big and thick, making her eyes seem bigger, and I knew that the person looking through them didn't mess around. Mrs. Lutzkraut may have been old, but she was no little old lady. She was built like a Chicago Bears middle line-backer. I instantly got the impression she wanted to drag me down the hall by my ear.

She glared at me for several more seconds, then

walked to the front of the line, turned, and uttered two sharp, crisp words. "Class! Enter!"

I was so scared I figured I'd better apologize for talking. "Mrs. Kraut-mouth," I blurted. The class burst out laughing.

"The name is LUTZkraut," she screamed, "and whoever you are, you'd better learn to shut your mouth."

"But I was just going to say that I was . . ."

"Silence!" Her voiced echoed off the walls. As we headed into class it was completely silent . . . except for Toby whispering in my ear, "You're dead, new kid."

Chapter 2

THE BIG FIGHT

Whenever I'm nervous, I say the completely wrong thing. It's an odd habit that's gotten me into a ton of trouble over the years. It was about to happen again. I could feel it welling up inside me. My new classroom was totally gray and depressing—gray walls, gray trim, gray shades pulled down to block the sun. As Mrs. Lutzkraut approached her desk, my mouth suddenly spoke out, "I love what you've done with the place." She stopped and spun in my direction, then stared down at me with a hideous scowl.

"What *is* your name?"

"Rodney Rathbone," I replied. I heard Toby snicker.

"Well, Mr. Rat-bone . . ."

"Rathbone," I corrected her. Everyone called me Rat-bone back in New York and I didn't want it repeated here. Rat-bone. Rat-boy. I had heard it all.

She glared at me for a moment, then yelled, "Don't

interrupt me! I've known you for three minutes and you're already one of the most irritating students I've ever had. Sit here." Her hand slapped an empty desk right in front of hers. "This morning we'll be discussing *my* rules and more importantly *my* punishments, two subjects to which you'd better pay close attention."

Super, I thought.

As the morning wore on, I came to truly understand how boring boredom could be. The more Mrs. Lutzkraut lectured us, the slower time seemed to pass, leaving me plenty of time to think. My mind kept returning to one question: *Could things get any worse?* I had gotten the bad teacher and the school thugs were out for me. Even though I was bored in class, I was in no hurry to leave and go to lunch. I didn't have any friends except Rishi and I wanted to hide from the two monsters I'd already met. My insides twisted when Mrs. Lutzkraut told us to line up and head down to the cafeteria.

A tall lunch aide with pulled-back hair and a nose that seemed to point all the way back to her forehead greeted me with, "Mrs. Lutzkraut's boys sit at table four." I noticed that Rishi had positioned himself as far from Toby as possible, so I sat down next to him.

"Who's that lady with the long nose?" I asked.

"Her? That's Long Nose. Hey, do you want to see a picture of my grandma's foot?" Rishi pulled out his camera.

"Uh, not really," I responded, wondering if my new friend had mental problems.

He laughed. "Hey, *now* let me introduce you to my buddies." Motioning to a heavy boy across from me he said, "This is Tim, but we call him Slim. And that," he pointed to a short, quiet-looking boy, "is Dave. We call him Dave." Rishi laughed again, and Slim and Dave said hello. Pretty soon the four of us were joking around and my nervousness over Josh, Toby, and Mrs. Lutzkraut faded. Maybe things would be okay after all.

Slim was busy telling about the time he laughed and soda came shooting out his nose. We were all laughing when he suddenly turned white and quickly looked down at his lunch. Something had caused him to react, and it didn't take a genius to figure out what, or who, was standing in back of me.

I turned around. Josh was there, with Toby a little behind. The long-nosed lunch lady was far away talking to other aides and not paying attention to the students. I gulped. Josh reached down and picked up my ham sandwich. "Toby here says you're a new kid. You lied to me on the bus."

"No, no I didn't. I thought you meant new to the United States. Like if I just moved here from Japan or Russia or something . . ."

"He's definitely a liar," Toby interrupted. "That's not a very nice thing to do, Rodn*eeeey*."

"I agree completely," I blubbered. "I was just saying to Rishi here how much I hate liars. . . ."

"Yeah, it isn't very nice to lie to me. I guess you and

me goin' to have a little talk about manners at recess." With that, Josh squeezed my sandwich in his fist. "Hey Toby," he asked, "how about a game of ham-ball?" They both laughed as he threw my sandwich halfway across the cafeteria into the side of some kid's face. The kid, who was drinking from a milk carton, had his head knocked back and milk went flying all over him and three of his friends. He whirled around and jumped up to see who had thrown it, ready for a fight. When he saw Josh and Toby laughing, he slowly turned back and started cleaning up the mess.

"I should be a pitcher. That was a perfect strike," Josh said. He looked back down at me and sneered, "I'll see you outside," and walked off.

Rishi, who had said nothing the whole time, said, "Too bad, Rodney. We probably would have liked you."

"What do you mean?"

"You're dead; that's what I mean." That was the second time this morning I had heard those words, and the worst part was that now I believed it. A minute later when we lined up for recess, my three new friends wished me good luck but moved away, not wanting to be near the recess sacrifice.

We filed out through the doors in the back of the cafeteria. Some kids bolted for the soccer field, others for the swings. Being a professional coward, I tore off in search of a place to hide for thirty minutes. I ran and ducked behind a big bush twice my size. My heart was pounding. I tried to peer through the bush, but it was too thick. I didn't want to stick my head out and get spotted, so I sat blindly, hiding, waiting.

I might have noticed them coming if I could see, but it was too late. The next thing I knew Toby walked around the corner and shouted, "Aha!" Panic gripped me and I took off in the other direction, running smack into Josh.

"Gotcha! Trying to hide? Well, you can't escape our talk. I think you need a lesson in manners. Isn't that right, Toby?"

Toby, who was behind me, answered with evil glee, "That's right. He should know lying isn't good manners." Other students noticed the three of us and gathered around. I wondered if this was the kind of excitement my dad was talking about. I'd be sure to tell him all about it later on in the emergency room—if I could, that is.

The crowd encircled us. "That's right!" Josh yelled, rolling his head back and forth. "Come see me learn the new kid some manners." I looked for the aides. They were in the distance talking and laughing, completely unaware that I was about to get beaten to a pulp. Frantically, I looked for any other adults that might help me, but all I saw was the high school baseball team practicing on a field on the other side of the fence. I heard the crack of a bat hitting a ball in the distance. A hard shove from Josh knocked me back to reality. This was it.

"So what'll it be, a black eye or a bloody nose?"

"What's the third choice?" I asked.

He looked confused. "Enough talking," he frowned. "Ready to die, new kid?" He pulled back his fist and took aim.

What a dumb question, I began to think, and then it happened . . . an event that was to change my life.

Some kid yelled, "Hey, look up there," but he didn't have to, because everyone was looking up anyway as five navy jets zoomed in low over our heads. Everyone looked up but me, that is. I was like a deer in the headlights, just staring straight ahead waiting for Josh's punch. And that's probably why I saw the ball—a mammoth home run from the high school team—coming straight our way, over the fence, flying like a bullet, sailing right toward us, and right at Josh!

It smashed him square in the nose with a loud crack and knocked him out before ricocheting away under the bush. With everyone looking up at the planes, no one but me—not even Josh—had seen the ball hit. As the jets sped away, the crowd's attention returned to the big fight. What they saw was Josh knocked out cold, sprawled at my feet with a bloody nose. Suddenly all eyes were on me. Then someone yelled, "Wow, the new kid knocked out Josh! He did it. Someone finally decked Josh!"

Chapter 3

MR. FEEBLETOP

Kids yelled in amazement. They patted me on the back and some cheered. For a moment I thought they might start singing, "Ding dong, the bully's dead. . . ."

After a few minutes my brain kicked into gear and I smiled to myself. When one kid asked how I did it, I responded with a relaxed, "It was nothing." This impressed them. I was now the kid to respect and maybe fear. One boy even acted out the fight. "It went like this," he announced. "Josh swung his fist down at the new kid. He . . ." (pointing at me) ". . . ducked and Josh missed, then he . . ." (again pointing at me) ". . . Hey, what's your name, anyway?"

"His name is Rodney, he's from New York, and he's with us." It was Rishi, who had popped up out of nowhere.

"Where'd you come from?" I whispered to him.

"What? We had your back all along," he replied, leaning over to take a picture of Josh.

"Really?" I asked.

"Well, I was prepared to collect your teeth," he said with a sly smile, "or write your mom a sad letter saying you died a brave death."

I smiled too. "Gee thanks, pal."

"Don't mention it."

Meanwhile the storyteller was still going on. "... Rodney then came up with this vicious right hook. It smashed into Josh's nose and he went down like a sack of potatoes. It was like Bam and Boom! What a punch!" Other kids chimed in saying that they'd seen it too. In every story I delivered some version of the greatest punch in playground history. Listening to them, I learned a valuable lesson. Don't say much, if anything. Say, "Oh, it was nothing," or, "I didn't do much." Stories sound a lot better and are more believable coming from someone else's mouth.

Everyone was all smiles until we were interrupted by a shriek. "Oh my goodness! Oh oh ahh . . ." Long Nose, the aide, had finally arrived on the scene. Kids scattered, leaving a couple of us standing over Josh, who was moaning and holding his nose. "Who did this?" she screamed. She was on the verge of hysterics and, glancing down at Josh, I noticed he did look gruesome. Another aide joined us and was bending over him. Long Nose asked again, this time more angrily than before, "Who *did* this?"

The other kids backed away. I knew I was going to

get it, but any punishment was better than saying the truth about the baseball. I raised my hand.

"You! New kid!" she snapped. "We don't hit at Baber Intermediate. Look what you did to that poor boy. You're going to the principal. We'll see what Mr. Feebletop has to say about this!" She grabbed my arm and off we went. Her ranting about my behavior and rudeness continued across the field, down the hall, and even as we walked into the main office. By the time she had me placed on a bench I wasn't just frightened, I was deaf.

She lowered her voice as she spoke to two secretaries but she still sounded upset. One of them went into the principal's office followed by Long Nose. I could hear them talking, interrupted by an occasional deep grunt. After a couple of minutes she flew by, sneering, "You little wretch. You're going to get it."

Now, waiting to speak to the principal is a scary thing. Thanks to my big mouth, I'd faced principals before and knew I was going to get some horrible speech and even worse punishment. The scariest part is that I knew nothing about this Mr. Feebletop. I craned my neck to see into his office. At that moment, an aide led a bleeding Josh into the nurse's office. The second he saw me, Josh jumped back and grabbed the nurse for protection. I almost laughed, but I heard the principal cough and remembered my immediate problems. Principals, after all, are the enforcers of the building, and fighting is always the worst thing you can do. "You may go in now," the secretary announced. I was about to meet my fate.

Mr. Feebletop had a frown on his large round face. He was big and bald with a very shiny head. His tie was loosened around his thick neck. He leaned in closer to his desk and looked at me with a serious expression. "Sit down," he said.

I walked over to a chair opposite him and as I sat I noticed a baseball on his desk, and that his walls were covered with photos of baseball players in orange and blue uniforms. The colors of the New York Mets, I thought. They were my hometown team. Behind his desk was a big framed picture of Tom Seaver, the great Mets pitcher. My mouth blurted out: "Tom Seaver." Again, it had acted on its own and was probably about to get me into even hotter water.

Mr. Feebletop spun around, stood up, and walked over to the picture. "You know about Tom Seaver?" he asked.

"He is the greatest Met of all time," I answered.

"You are completely right about that," he almost yelled. "They should never have traded him. Ahhhh, that was the team. The '69 Mets."

"They were great in 1986, too," I said. "Keith Hernandez was an awesome first baseman." My dad was a big Mets fan and had made me watch a number of the old classic games.

"He was one of the best," Mr. Feebletop agreed. Then

a big grin spread across his face. "So you know about Keith Hernandez, huh? They just don't make them like that anymore, do they? He was the finest defensive first baseman of the twentieth century."

From this point on, Mr. Feebletop launched into a history of the team. At times, I mentioned little things I knew. How long we sat there I'm not sure, but one thing was certain. Not since Christmas morning had I seen anyone so happy. Eventually, a secretary stuck her head in.

"Excuse me, Mr. Feebletop. Mrs. Panic wants to talk to you about her chorus schedule."

"Oh, uh, okay," he answered. He looked back at me. "Well, it was great meeting you . . ."

"Rodney."

"Ah yes, Rodney. We should do this again. Oh . . ." He paused. ". . . Let me think. Oh yes, you were fighting, right? Well, hmmm. Try not to do it again. Oh hey, did you see my Tom Seaver baseball?"

"I did. It's great," I answered.

He smiled at me as I walked out of his office. I could hear him mumbling to himself, "A nice boy, a nice boy."

Chapter 4

MY NEW REPUTATION

I couldn't believe my luck. The bully hadn't pounded me, I had gotten credit for knocking him out, and I had escaped without a major punishment! Back in class the kids all looked excited and smiled at me. Rishi yelled, "Rodney Balboa!" and I raised my arms like the champ.

"Silence, Rishi," hollered Mrs. Lutzkraut, smacking her hand down on top of her desk. "And you, sit down!" She jumped up from her chair and was in front of my desk with her finger pointing at my nose. "I have taught many years," she began. For a second my mouth started to say, "That's obvious," but I managed to clamp it shut. She continued, "And in all my years I have never had anyone behave so badly, act so rudely, and care so little as you. You managed to do this all in one day. You can join me for recess this week and the next, and I promise you, your parents will know all about your behavior when I phone them later. Do you understand?"

"Yes."

She was breathing hard and staring at me. Eventually she returned to her desk and I exhaled. She sure knew how to take the thrill out of my victory. In fact, I started to feel sorry for myself and was worrying about what would happen when my parents found out. Then I started worrying about Toby and the bus ride home. I looked around the class and suddenly noticed something a lot more interesting than Toby. A real pretty blond girl was looking right at me. She mouthed the words, "Are you all right?"

I nodded and thought, *Now I am*.

For the rest of the afternoon I spent my time focused on her until Mrs. Lutzkraut announced it was time to line up for the buses. We trudged down the hallway, my nervousness growing with each step. I saw my bus and reluctantly climbed aboard.

A rowdy cheer greeted me. Kids clapped and waved, and all over the bus they hollered, "Sit here!" or "Great job, Rodney!"

The one boy not yelling was the one I had been worrying about. He sat in the seat right behind the driver, cowering. Any closer and he'd be sitting in the driver's lap. I smiled to myself. Without Josh, Toby wasn't a danger. I would later find out I was wrong about that, but for now he was on his best behavior.

I made my way to the back of the bus, where Rishi motioned for me to join him. "I have taken the liberty of reserving the preferred back seat for you, sir," he said, acting like a snooty waiter. He snapped his fingers. "Slim, wipe it down."

Like a busboy, Slim jumped up and wiped the seat with his backpack. "The previous customer who occupied this seat," he explained, "was met by an unfortunate accident at recess and may never sniff again. I hope you have better luck. Can I get you something to drink?"

"Yeah, root beers all around," I joked. Rishi laughed and sat down. We happily discussed the fight and made fun of Toby sniveling in the front. I looked around the bus and realized what a difference a day makes. Unfortunately, I knew I wouldn't be enjoying such a great welcome once back at home, thanks to Mrs. Lutzkraut.

When I got there, however, my mom greeted me with a big smile, asking, "So how was your first day of school?"

"Uh, fine, I guess." I couldn't believe it. Maybe Mrs. Lutzkraut wasn't all that bad. Maybe she just pretended to act mean in front of the class.

"And how was your teacher?" my mom asked. *Brrriiiinnngggg!!* The phone interrupted her. She picked up the receiver and I cringed. "Hello," she said. "Yes, hi, how are you? . . . Oh . . . Really? . . . Well, I—I can't believe he'd . . . Taken to the *hospital*? . . . Yes, I understand it's very serious. . . . I understand . . . I am very sorry about this, we'll certainly talk to him. . . . Yes, we'll punish him too . . . . Yes, severely . . . Yes, okay, I'll talk to you soon. . . . Sorry . . . Okay, bye," and with that she hung up. My mom held her chest for a second. "Rodney, get to your room. Just wait till your father gets home."

About an hour later I heard him walk in. In less than a minute I was being summoned downstairs. Sitting in front of both my parents, I was asked to explain what had happened, which I did, leaving out the baseball.

"So, you punched him in the nose?" my dad asked.

"Yes."

"He had his friend with him?"

"Yes," I replied again.

"So, you're saying you took on two bullies, and you knocked one out?"

"Uh, yeah . . . that's what happened."

My dad then stood up and I got ready for the lecture. I hated his talks. They could be threatening but, worse than that, they had a way of making me feel guilty. He was good at it, and both my mother and I waited.

Strangely, he didn't say anything. He started throwing imaginary punches in the air. "Gave him the old Rathbone Hook, did you?" He was now ducking and weaving like Muhammad Ali.

"Donald! Donald, your son hit a boy today, and you're, you're . . . What are you doing?"

"Honey," my dad turned to my mother, "a boy has to defend himself."

"But . . ."

"Sweetie, you were never a boy, and there are times you have to fight."

"Well, I don't think encouraging . . ."

"Honey Bunny, no one's encouraging anything. He defended himself, and that is what a boy sometimes has to do. Maybe he should take boxing lessons. He may be a real talent."

"Absolutely not!" My mom ended it, and a good thing, too. I doubted my real right hook could knock out a pigeon.

My parents left me in the den. My smile faded when my sister, Penny, walked in. "You won a fight?" she asked.

"Yes," I said.

She gave me a look that made me uneasy. "How did *that* happen?" she asked. "I thought you were scared of everyone. Last year, didn't that second grader chase you all the way home?"

I remembered the nasty second grader with a shiver. How was I to know he was holding a lollipop and not a club? Of course, I wasn't about to admit that to Penny, who was only eight but too smart for *my* own good. "No, that was a race. Which I won, I might add."

She rolled her eyes.

"Isn't it your bedtime?" I asked, shoving her out of the den.

Later that night, I lay in bed staring at the ceiling with my head resting on my hands. I thought about the day. It was awesome. Overall, things couldn't be better. I would soon find out, however, that it's harder to maintain an excellent reputation than it is to get one.

Chapter 5

THE McTHUGG BROTHERS

When people believe you have a right hook like a heavyweight champ, life is pretty good. It's even better when you use that famous punch to knock out public enemy number one. As soon as Josh crumpled to the dirt, Baber Intermediate became a new place. I didn't realize it at first, since I had never gone there before, but over the next couple of weeks it became clear. That nose-seeking baseball had saved my skin—and everyone else's.

"This is the first time I like school," Dave announced one morning as we lined up for class.

"Yeah, I get to eat my whole lunch now," Slim added. "Josh used to always eat my Doritos and cupcakes."

"That was probably a good thing," Rishi joked, patting Slim's belly. "You're right, though," he continued. "This year sure is nice, and we owe it all to our main man here."

Then he pointed at Josh and Toby. "How ya feeling

today, Josh? Got the sniffles? Must be tough to blow your nose?"

Oh no. Josh looked back at us. He had returned to school just a few days earlier and his face was still black and blue. His nose, which was covered by a large splint, now made a strange whistling noise when he breathed. Even though I hadn't said anything, he was staring straight at me.

"Looking good!" Rishi yelled.

Will you shut up, I thought. Josh and Toby were still afraid of me since the supposed fight, but I didn't want to get them mad enough to try something again.

Rishi was convinced I would bail him out of any trouble. His big mouth scared me, but we had become best friends, along with Slim and Dave. I still missed my old friends from New York, but thanks to these guys I was having a lot of fun at my new school.

There was someone else I liked a lot, but in a different way. I found myself thinking about that pretty blond girl in my class. Her name was Jessica. She looked great and seemed nice, but she was best friends with Kayla—a girl whose favorite hobby was rolling her eyes, making nasty faces, and keeping Jessica to herself.

On two wonderful days when Kayla was out with strep throat, Jessica and I did speak, and it went well. After that she would sometimes look right at me and smile, which was great, except that my face would turn red. Rishi would usually show up at these moments and make some gross kissing noises. Sometimes I'd tackle him, but I was really in such a good mood that I didn't mind all that much.

Yes, most things were good. Really good. An e-mail from New York reminded me just how good. The e-mail was from Timmy, one of my three best friends back in New York. It said:

> I hope you're having fun in Ohio. Things here are the same. Rocco punched me, elbowed Tony, and smacked Tommy. Talk to you later.

Rocco. Reading his name made me wince. His full name was Rocco Salvatore Ronboni. One time a rather unintelligent kid made fun of his name. He said, "Hey Ronzoni, make me some spaghetti!" Those were his final words. We never saw him again. Some said he moved away, but most of us pictured darker outcomes. Instead we kept our mouths shut tight and tried our best to avoid Rocco, the worst bully in New York City.

Knowing his atomic wedgies, full nelsons, and locker-room headlocks were five hundred miles away was comforting, but I felt bad for my boys. Timmy, Tony, and Tommy hadn't benefited from the baseball incident like me and were still taking daily beatings.

As I sat and thought about them, I knew more than ever that my phony tough-guy rep meant everything to my survival. My sister had said it was only a matter of time before the true Rodney was discovered. With a shiver I wondered if life at Baber might take a turn for the worse, and that's exactly what happened one chilly day in late September.

Like most Americans, my friends and I watched football on Sundays. After school we'd meet at a vacant field by my house and try to re-create the great plays of the pros. It belonged to an elementary school that was now closed and boarded up, but it was a perfect place to play since the school district still mowed the lawn. We arranged to meet there at four o'clock.

As I ran out the door my mom yelled, "Get back here, mister!" I turned. "You're not ruining another good school shirt. Here, put this on." She held up a light blue jersey. On the front was a big picture of Mickey Mouse.

"Mom, Mickey? I'm a little old to be running around with . . ."

"I don't care. I picked this up at a garage sale. It doesn't matter if you rip or stain it. Put it on." I sighed, but did what she said. Right before I left, she added, "Bet it brings you good luck." Little did she know how much I would need it.

I rode my bike up to the field and saw there were already kids running around and throwing balls to each other. Rishi saw me and muttered, "Nice shirt," before turning to the crowd. "All right, let's make teams . . ."

"Hey, you punks! Get off our lawn!" It was a deep

angry voice and it was coming through a crack in the stockade fence. We all froze and waited.

"Let's just see if he goes away," Rishi whispered.

Even though we were on public property, the guy doing the yelling was a McThugg, and you didn't want to argue with him. I had first heard about the McThuggs from Rishi. They were four brothers who were either in their twenties or thirties and roamed the streets of Garrettsville, my new hometown. They were famous for terrorizing anyone who got in their way. Their house was next to where we played ball, and most of the time they didn't bother us because they were out causing trouble down at the Silver Crik Saloon. When they were in their backyard, however, we knew to stay away from their fence. They didn't seem to like anyone or anything—except their Harleys and loud music.

"Are you punks deaf?" the voice suddenly shouted again. "That's it, I'm coming over!"

We took off and ran around the corner of the building, where we could hide but still keep an eye on the field. Engines revved and dark smoke floated up over the fence, but so far no one was coming. We waited, almost afraid to talk to each other. After five minutes, Slim complained, "This is crazy. I'm going to have to leave soon for dinner."

"Figures, you're already thinking of dinner," Rishi teased him.

"Well yeah, but I'm also thinking about what

happened the last time, when the McThuggs came around the fence and tried to run us over with their motorcycles."

I was beginning to question whether football was worth it today, but things eventually quieted down and Rishi suggested we head back to the grass. Once there, we made teams and were about to start playing when two more kids rode up on their bikes. I almost left when I saw them. What were Josh and Toby doing here? As Josh hung back on his bike, Toby came over and stood in front of us on the field. "Can I play?" he asked.

Everyone stopped and looked at me. *Terrific,* I thought. They want the chicken to handle this. Believe me, I wanted to say no, but I was scared of what he might do. With everyone looking to me for a decision, I said, "Let him play." It was my first bad move of the afternoon.

We played for a while. I did okay, considering the fact that I couldn't decide who to fear most, Josh and Toby or the McThuggs. What happened next didn't exactly clear up my confusion.

Chapter 6

THE BRAIN and THE BEES

Strange as it seems, Toby was apparently ignorant of the dangers lurking on the other side of the fence. He must have been, because he suddenly suggested, "We should move the game closer to the fence. Too many rocks over here."

I should have realized right away what was happening.

"No way!" shouted Dave.

"Are you crazy?" Slim yelled.

"Toby, don't you know what's on the other side of that fence?" Rishi asked. "We can't play any closer to the McThugg brothers."

"They're not paying attention to us," Toby told Rishi. Then he looked right at me. "Besides, we have every right to be here—unless you're chicken."

In the corner of my eye I noticed Jessica, Kayla, and Samantha. They had come down to watch us play. Trying to sound cool and confident, I told Toby, "Let's move the game over, then. I'm not afraid of some loudmouth bikers."

That satisfied everyone. We walked over to the fence and Toby spoke up again. "Hey, let me be quarterback." He was on the other team so I didn't care much who threw the ball. On the next play Dave ran an out toward the fence. Toby faded back and threw a pass toward him. The pass may have gone in Dave's general direction but it went twenty feet over his head. We all watched it. I remember thinking for a moment that it was a nice spiral. It seemed to hang in the air for a few seconds before disappearing on the other side of the fence—right into the McThuggs' lair. I doubted we'd see it again.

Then I remembered that it was no ordinary ball. Rishi's uncle worked for the Browns and had just given him the new ball. In fact, Rishi had proudly shown it to everyone in class that very morning, pointing out that it was a real NFL football. Now it was gone. Rishi held his hands to his face with a look of complete anguish, only able to mumble, "Foot . . . foot . . . foot . . ."

"What's the matter with your foot?" Slim asked.

But Rishi didn't answer. Instead he exploded at Toby. "You threw it over the fence! You did it on purpose!"

Toby stood with a slight frown. "I didn't throw it on purpose. My hand slipped."

Rishi said, "What am I going to do now? You owe me a ball!"

"I ain't givin' you nothin'. Besides, it ain't that big of a de—"

"Not a big deal?" Rishi screamed.

Toby put a hand up and said, "Wait. There's an easy solution."

"What solution?" Rishi asked, and the rest of us wondered the same thing. We leaned in closer to hear what he had to say. If I knew what was coming, I'd have slunk away in the other direction. I definitely wasn't prepared for Toby's response.

"Think about it, Rishi. We have Rodney standing right here." I didn't like the sound of my name popping up. "He's like the bravest and toughest kid in Garrettsville. He can go get it. Besides, he said he wasn't afraid of the McThuggs."

My heart almost stopped, and I cursed my big mouth. I waited for Rishi and the other kids to yell that he was crazy, that no one could go into the McThuggs' yard. To my growing alarm, no one said anything. All eyes were on me, including the three girls' and, worst of all, Josh's, who had joined us on the field the moment Rishi's ball went over the fence.

For the first time I realized that my reputation for bravery could have a bad side. In this case a very bad side—four crazy brothers who would just love to torture some dopey kid who had wandered into their yard.

To my horror, Rishi even smiled a little, believing that Toby had solved his problem. "Boy, Rodney. I'm sure glad you're here."

What was he talking about? He actually believed I should go in there? For a football? I couldn't speak.

Maybe the kids mistook my silence for coolness, because the next thing I knew they began pulling an old metal garbage can toward the fence. "Let me help," Josh offered.

I tried hard to think of a way to weasel out of it, but I could just imagine what Jessica would think of me. No doubt Kayla would spin my wimp-out story tomorrow for the whole school.

I gulped. Then I noticed Toby and Josh smiling at each other, like they were enjoying a secret, and I realized Rishi had been right. That high pass was no accident. Toby probably had planned it the second he saw the new football in Mrs. Lutzkraut's class.

Figuring this all out did nothing to help me. I walked toward the garbage can. Maybe there'd be some escape route on the other side. With shaking hands I climbed on top, grabbed the fence, and pulled up. Just then I heard Jessica yell, "We should call the cops."

I dangled, listening. Finally, a voice of reason. When no one said anything she continued, a bit less sure of herself, "Well, just in case. You know . . ."

Sadly it was followed by Rishi. "Jessica, they wouldn't come. The cops are afraid of the McThuggs. But don't worry, those brothers have finally met their match. Go to it, Rodney!"

A cold late-day wind blew against my face and I noticed that the sun was already going down. I balanced with the top of the fence between my armpits and elbows and peered over. The yard was a complete disaster. Junk was everywhere. There were tires and old cars and gutters lying in a rusty pile. Grass grew up around moldy sofas left out in the rain. The only thing that was taken care of was a row of polished, shiny motorcycles. I gulped. The McThuggs were home. But where? Then I noticed it, looking very small and far away, down in the back corner of the yard in front of the crumbling garage. Rishi's prized football.

The kids behind me were quiet. By now there were at least thirty of them. One kid ran away, he was so scared.

How long I balanced up there I still have no idea, but time seemed to slow. I noticed that the wooden gate leading to the front yard was closed. It was probably as far from the ball as possible. After a brief prayer, I swiveled my legs over the stockade top, balanced on the wooden post, and lowered myself into the yard of death.

It wasn't bravery that made me jump. I don't have any of that running through my veins. It was my fear of life retuning to the way it had been in my last school. I couldn't let Josh become the next Rocco Ronboni. I had to climb over, but once on the ground I realized I had made a bad decision. The fence, without the aid of a garbage can and other kids to boost me up, was too high to climb. I looked up and began to shake. The day's lunch slid up into my throat. I turned around, expecting the McThuggs to be standing there, but they weren't.

After a couple of seconds, I tiptoed toward the garage and the ball.

I came around an old car and I could see the ball clearly now. Maybe I'd make it. Glancing sideways, I went up to the ball and bent over to pick it up. As I grabbed it my heart stopped. Standing five feet from me were three heavily tattooed men in the garage. I choked down a scream, then realized that they were all busy looking down at some motorcycle part and hadn't noticed me. All I had to do was tiptoe the other way and I'd be fine. . . .

"How's it GOING in there?" Rishi suddenly screamed from behind the fence. The three of them spun around.

"Uhhh," was all that dribbled out of my mouth.

Two of the brothers snarled and started toward me while the other one turned and grabbed something. "You breakin' in?" growled one guy, now coming closer. He had a big bald head, a lightning-bolt tattoo on his neck, and a goatee.

"M-me? I was j-just trying to g-get our football," I stammered, backpedaling.

"Football? I told you to get off our lawn," said the one nearest me. He had long black, greasy hair that was tied back by an orange bandanna. "Did you think I was kidding? Do you know what happened to the last guy who didn't listen to me?" The third brother had joined them and was holding something shiny and metal in his hand. They were circling me now and my knees were wiggling.

"You trying to steal our motorcycles?" the bald one snapped.

"Motorcycles? I can barely ride a bike!" I said.

"Hey look, the kid's got a rat on his shirt!" the one with the greasy hair yelled, pointing to my chest.

The bald one looked down. "You're right! That is a rat." He reached out and gripped the front of my shirt in his hands. "You a Ratfield boy?"

"A who?" I wheezed.

"Don't play dumb. Our family's been battling those low-down dirty Ratfields for years, and you just stroll in here wearing that rat shirt."

"It's Mickey Mouse. . . ."

"Who?" the bald one barked. I realized these guys were one dumb bunch of lug nuts. But dumb as they were, they were also the scariest guys I'd ever met.

Greasy Hair said, "He's definitely a Ratfield. They must think they're pretty smart sending a kid to do their dirty work. Well, kid, you didn't get the drop on us. We is too smart for that."

Baldy added, "We better send them a message. Show 'em what we do to little spies. What do you think we should do with him?"

"Why don't we ask the Brain?"

"Good idea. Go get the Brain and tell him to come out here." For a moment, my panic level dipped. With a brother called the Brain coming out, maybe I'd be saved. Surely this guy would see that I wasn't a spy or a Ratfield and let me go. I started to exhale, but within a minute the back door slammed, and when the Brain walked into the fading afternoon light I almost threw up.

He was well over six feet tall and had more muscles than I'd ever seen. His black tank top was stained with what looked like blood. I looked up at his face. His eyes were dark, crazy, and angry. He had a large bone pierced through his nose, and I knew nothing was going to save me.

The bald one, smiling evilly, said, "What do you think we should do with this here Ratfield?"

The Brain glared at me before picking up a bottle and smashing it over his own head.

"Now you know why we call him the Brain. And he . . ." I didn't wait to hear more about the Brain. My legs, full of nervous energy, rocketed off. The bald one still had my shirt in his hands and I heard it rip but my feet kept moving.

The McThuggs took off after me. I ran blindly down an aisle of junk, weaving in and out of old washing machines, piles of bricks, and even a wooden Indian statue. I turned left between a Buick and a sofa and thought for a second that I was cornered. Seeing a gap, I ran and did a baseball slide right under an open car door, almost dropping the football. The Brain didn't need to slide. He just ran through it, the rusty metal hinges tearing off the car's frame. The door slowed him temporarily, and I sprinted and hurdled my way through the junk to the far-off opening.

As I ran toward the gate, I noticed a padlock hanging from a rusty latch. I didn't have time to think. Instead I lowered my shoulder and ran as hard as I could into the gate. There was a loud bang. I fell back to the ground, and landing next to me was the biggest wasps' nest I'd ever seen. The fall had cracked it open and hundreds of furious yellow jackets came scrambling out. I slammed myself into the gate again. This time the rusty hinge came loose and it swung open. I ran out and slammed the gate behind me.

I backed away toward the road. A loud, deep, angry buzz filled the air. And then, "AHHHHHHHHHHH! Beees! Ahhh ooaaaa oaw! Ooooch! Owwww Owwwww. I'm getting out of here!" The McThuggs were screaming and cursing. The gate opened partway, with the bald one swinging wildly at the air, screaming like a baby.

Hearing the commotion, the football gang tore over to the chain-link fence that separated the field from the sidewalk. They arrived in time to hear moans of agony. Then they flinched as one McThugg ran past them, shrieking, crying, and flailing his arms around his head like the devil himself had chased him.

"Save me!" he screamed as he turned the corner. Three more brothers followed him. As my friends looked back down the block to see what had scared the town's most dangerous criminals so badly, they saw me standing there, dirty, shirt ripped, holding the prized football.

They went bananas. They scrambled over or around the chain-link fence and rushed toward me. Instantly, I found myself being hoisted up on shoulders while the cheering mob carried me down the street.

"He beat the McThuggs with his bare hands!" one kid was shouting.

"That's what I'm talking about," Rishi exclaimed as he took my picture.

I smiled down at him and flipped him the ball. Kayla just rolled her eyes and walked off, but I remember thinking as we rounded the corner onto the field that no running back, not Walter Payton or even Jim Brown, had ever made such a brilliant football run. In the distance I saw Josh and Toby pedaling away as fast as they could. From time to time they looked back to make sure I wasn't coming for them.

Chapter 7

THE LEGEND OF OLD MAN JOHNSON

By the time I arrived at school the next day, my victory over the McThuggs had spread far and wide. The bus was abuzz with it. We were, of course, silent around Mrs. Lutzkraut, but at art, with Mr. Borus, the stories began again. Mr. Borus himself told of a time the McThuggs had circled his minivan and had threatened him for twelve blocks.

By the next day, the tale had grown to the point that Mr. Feebletop himself mentioned it in the morning announcements. He talked about famous heroes and bravery and then related it by saying: "We here at Baber are fortunate enough to have seen bravery in action. Someone in this town finally stood up to a group that's menaced our town for years. Well done, Rodney! Now rise for the pledge."

As we made the familiar speech with our hands on our hearts, Mrs. Lutzkraut sneered at me. When we sat down she said, "I don't think there's anything brave about doing something as stupid as you did. First off, you were trespassing. Secondly, other children will now approach strangers. You can join me for recess and write an essay explaining why your actions were wrong. I'll talk to Mr. Feebletop about letting you read it over the loudspeaker tomorrow."

Rishi interjected, "Mrs. Lutzkraut, Rodney was . . ."

"Rishi! Save your energy for math! Boys and girls, take out your textbooks, notebooks, and put a heading . . ." I looked around. Rishi was angrily taking out a book. Jessica was busy writing something. Unfortunately, she wasn't busy looking at me, which was strange, since she had been there when I supposedly had throttled the McThuggs. I worried that maybe Kayla had begun to poison her mind against me. And as for Toby, he hadn't said a word since I climbed the fence. Sitting next to me, he looked pale and sick and was clearly avoiding eye contact. In all the excitement, I hadn't given him much thought. But I had seen that smile he had given Josh as I walked to my fate. Toby was out to get me.

"Rodney!"

"Yes, Mrs. Lutzkraut?" I choked.

"What is the answer to number five?"

Apparently we were checking the math homework. "Um, forty-two," I guessed.

She smiled. For a second I thought I had it right. Then she continued, "No! You're not even remotely close. I suppose the famous McThuggs ate your homework while they chased you down the . . ."

"Actually, I chased them," I corrected her.

"Silence! The day's just started and I've already had enough of you." She stared at me long and hard before moving on to the next question.

Halloween, my least-favorite holiday, was fast approaching. Yes, I like the candy, but there are many other things about it that don't quite work for a scaredy-cat like me. First off, I hate the dressing up part. I don't mind seeing Superman or a few fairy princess costumes but I can definitely do without the Draculas and Freddy Kruegers.

Last year, Rocco Ronboni cornered me along with his posse as I walked the streets of my old neighborhood with Timmy, Tony, and Tommy. He yelled, "Fire!" and blasted me in the face with shaving cream. "Hey Rathbone, how does that feel?" He laughed. I recalled my eyes beginning to burn. "Hey, check it out, guys," he had continued. "This shaving cream contains menthol. Avoid contact with the eyes. Whoops!" I remembered their laughs as I stumbled blindly along Bell Boulevard. Well, at least he was far away now. Maybe, with Josh and Toby leaving me alone, I'd coast through Halloween this year with no problems.

I would soon discover, however, that in Garrettsville, Halloween isn't easily avoided. The kids began talking about costumes and candy even before September came to a close. Some of them started collecting secret stashes of shaving cream or Silly String. I made a mental note to get a costume with protective eyewear. Stories of eggs flying and paintballs shooting were quietly discussed in the back of the bus. But I didn't learn of the town's main horror until one afternoon in mid-October.

I finished my homework, grabbed my football, and walked out the door. Rishi and Slim were waiting for me on their bikes. They looked kind of nervous or something. "We're going for a bike ride before we play football," Rishi explained.

"Uh, okay, sounds nice," I replied. Slim giggled nervously.

"Get your wheels and we'll get Dave," Rishi yelled as he rode off. "Meet us at the end of the block."

It was a nice autumn day. A ride seemed like a good idea, but Rishi and Slim were acting a bit off, and my chicken sense was tingling. I noticed my palms sweating as I pulled my bike from the garage.

When we all linked up, the three of them were even stranger. Dave muttered a quiet, "Hey Rodney," and we were off, winding down streets and cutting through paths. We passed Crystal Lake and, as we made a right onto Elm Street, the pace slowed. Somehow, the street felt darker. The houses looked bleak and run-down. The grass wasn't as green and there were no people walking around. Then, in the distance, I could see a house that made my stomach gurgle, and I wished there was a bathroom nearby. Somehow I knew it was where we were going, and anger and panic swept through me. "Why are you bringing me here?" I asked in the steadiest voice I could manage.

"You'll see, Rodney. Just a little closer," Rishi answered.

The house was menacing. It was boarded up and decrepit. The paint was peeling and dirty. It must have been white years ago, but now it was grayish brown. The green roof was missing tiles and was full of holes. The porch looked sinister and the railing was missing spindles. Two old lions, chipped and dirty, sat at either side of the walkway like they were guarding the place.

I had trouble swallowing. My hands quivered and I hoped no one was looking at me. We rode up to the curb and the four of us stood looking at the den of evil. "It's Old Man Johnson's house," Rishi said. "He murdered his whole family."

"I heard the house is possessed," Slim said. I fully believed him. It seemed to be looking down at me, with the top two windows like eyes and the downstairs windows forming an eerie grin.

"I thought we lived in Garrettsville, not Amityville," I muttered. They looked at me, slightly confused, but their attention returned to the house as an old swing out back screeched in the light breeze and a shutter banged against the siding. I no longer cared about my tough guy reputation. Rishi beat me to it and yelled,

"Let's get out of here!" We all tore behind him, and it wasn't until we were safely at our football field near the vacant elementary school that we stopped pedaling. The McThugg brothers, by the way, hadn't bothered us since the wasp incident. Evidently, they thought I had brought the yellow-jacket bees with me that day as a warning from the Ratfields.

"So," Rishi turned to us breathing hard, "who's going to do it this year?" I didn't know what he was talking about, but I knew I didn't like whatever "it" was. I tossed the football onto the grass and got off my bike.

"What's the deal?" I asked. "What's this 'it' you're talking about?"

Rishi looked me in the eyes and said, "Rodney, that's where we're going on Halloween night." I figured I'd correct him on that one. He might be going there but I wasn't going anywhere near the place.

"I won't be able to join you, I have . . ."

Slim interrupted me. "Rodney, you got to go. Every year something scary and exciting happens at Old Man Johnson's house. You can't miss it."

"Have you gone?"

"Well no, but my older brother Charlie said it's the thing to do in Garrettsville. And besides, he wouldn't let us go last year, but now he'll let us go because he wants to meet you. He says they're all talking about you in high school and what you did to the McThuggs."

Talking about me in high school? What was next, my own show on the Disney Channel?

Rishi jumped in. "Look, Rodney, none of us have ever gone, but now that you're with us, we'll be all right. Besides, every year someone tries to get close to the house and do something crazy. . . ."

"Yeah, and you're just the guy," Dave added, but I cut him off. *Crazy* wasn't my idea of a great Halloween.

"That's nice, you go be crazy, but my mom makes me take my sister out, so I probably won't be able to go with you. Too bad, though. It sounds exciting."

"Don't worry," Rishi said, as he put a hand on my shoulder. "We'll wait for you to finish. This is something I know that someone as tough as you, someone who lives for danger, would not want to miss."

Oh man! I didn't know what to say to get out of it. "Uh, okay," I mumbled, and then, trying to get back to nicer things, I asked, "Still time for football today?"

We all thought about it but it was already getting late, so we said good-bye and rode off. It wasn't until I was on my street that I remembered the football. I had left it in the field by the school. The sky was dark orange, and night was coming on, so I raced back as fast as I could.

By the time I got to the school it was almost dark out and the chilly air smelled like leaves. No one was around and I found myself alone on the empty field with the abandoned building sitting quietly in the distance. The place sure was creepy. Something seemed to move in the shadows by the building. As I reached for the football I thought I saw a guy with a hockey mask peering down at me from one of the upper windows. With my imagination running wild, it wasn't long before my feet did too, and I pedaled home full speed. If I couldn't even be alone on a field for five seconds, what would happen to me on Halloween?

That night I slept with the light on, thinking of escape plans and hoping Old Man Johnson was safely behind bars—not lurking behind the walls of his house.

Chapter 8

A GHOSTLY ENCOUNTER

Everyone dressed up for Halloween at Baber. In New York we weren't allowed to dress up in school, which suited me fine, but that was not the case here. Apparently, Mr. Feebletop loved Halloween as much as the kids, and everyone was in full costume as they arrived that Thursday morning.

Dressed as Babe Ruth, Mr. Feebletop waited at the front door inspecting and applauding costumes as they passed by. I was dressed up as a football player. Rishi was Darth Vader. Dave and Slim were mummies, although their costumes had pretty much unraveled by the time they got to class. Mrs. Lutzkraut was the only one not dressed. "I love her costume," Rishi whispered to me.

"Yeah, she makes a perfect witch," I shouted back. Oops.

Mrs. Lutzkraut spun around. She swung her ruler in the air angrily, and for a moment I really believed she was weaving an evil spell. Actually it was almost as bad.

"Rodney, you'll add two more weeks of recess with me for that one." Ugh. "And as for the rest of you, hurry and get unpacked. If the costumes prove too distracting to our lessons, there'll be no Halloween party at the end of the day."

I tried to focus, but it's hard adding mixed numbers in shoulder pads. Amazingly, though, we did have a party that day, but I soon wished we hadn't, for that's when things started to go badly.

Toby had been quiet since his little plan to get me killed by the McThuggs had failed. Now, Rishi did his best to wake him up. Walking through the party in full Darth Vader clothing and mask, he approached Toby, who wore a fake mustache and a brown derby hat. He grabbed him by the shoulders and said, "Toby-Wan Kenobi . . . I am your father." A bunch of us laughed. The only person not smiling was Toby-Wan.

"Yeah, you're havin' fun now, but let's see who's smiling tonight at Old Man Johnson's. I heard you were heading down there."

"That's right," Rishi shot back. "We'll be there, and we'll see who goes farther up the steps to the . . ."

"Look," I interrupted, wanting to change the subject. "Mrs. Lutzkraut is giving out bags of candy."

Sure enough, she had pulled a large bag from her closet and placed it on her desk. She cleared her throat and began, "I want you to sit down. I prepared a little party treat. Several days ago I made each of you an egg-salad sandwich." I gagged and dropped my head onto the desk.

The day and the party eventually ended. Mrs. Lutzkraut gave us a stack of homework and reminded us to study for the science test tomorrow morning. Homework on Halloween! She definitely made an excellent witch.

"I'm tired," my sister whined. I had already dragged her to about a hundred houses.

"Oh come on, Penny, a few more. Just think of all the candy!"

"I don't care," she whined. "My feet hurt. I want to go home."

I could see she was about done and I figured that my friends had probably left by now without me. Then I reconsidered. "Let's hit Oak Street before heading back."

"Just 'cause you're too scared to go out with your friends, you don't have to torture me."

"Scared? Me? Seriously, Penny, where do you come up with this stuff? I just enjoy spending time with you." She wasn't buying any of it and shook her head as I walked her home, as slowly as I could. Everything seemed quiet as we climbed the porch steps. I let out a little sigh of relief as I turned the knob and entered the front door.

Then I jumped. Three hooligans in dark outfits were waiting for me. Actually it was only Slim, Dave, and

Rishi talking to my mom, but I think I would have preferred hooligans.

"So, where are you going?" my mom asked Rishi.

"We're just heading around. Get some candy. Show Rodney the Halloween spots."

"Rodney's afraid to go out. He's especially scared of shaving cream. . . ." Penny's big mouth started up but stopped just as quickly when she saw me reach for the sofa cushion. I had found that threatening to smother her was an effective way to shut her up.

"My sister's always the joker. You know, shaving cream, it's the menthol . . . reacts poorly with my sensitive skin . . . got hives this one time . . . yeah, not fun . . ." I was mumbling through the excuse until I realized no one was paying attention.

My mom changed the subject. "Penny, go brush your teeth. After all that candy, we don't want any more cavities. And, boys, don't get back late. You have school tomorrow."

"We won't, Mrs. Rathbone," Rishi answered. Slim grabbed me by the shoulder and we headed out into the October night. The air wasn't too cold and I was happy to see how bright the night had become—until I realized it was due to a scary full moon on the rise.

The four of us walked down the various streets. Some kids were running around having fun. Obviously they weren't heading in the direction of Old Man Johnson's home. As for us, our conversations were thin and quiet. Slim looked white and hadn't said much of anything. Dave was talking to Rishi about eggs or something, although neither seemed real interested in what they were saying. A sense of dread hung over us.

Eventually we turned onto Elm Street. A crowd of kids had gathered several lots from the Johnson house. Most of the kids looked nervous or scared. One kid said, "Oh good, Rodney's here," as if I was going to somehow protect him. I tried hard to control my leg from shaking and slowly shuffled my way to the back of the crowd. Trouble, though, in the form of Toby, soon found me.

"There you are. I thought you guys wouldn't show," he exclaimed.

I noticed Josh standing behind him in a leather jacket with silver rivets sticking out from the shoulders and sleeves. He was quiet, angry looking, and serious. Some kid in a mask who I didn't recognize said, "What did you think? Rodney's not going to miss something like this."

What a fool, I thought.

Toby looked at me, but perhaps thinking about my legendary punching ability, turned to Rishi. "There's no way you guys are heading up to the house. I can see it in your eyes."

"I don't see you standing up there," Rishi said. Then he threw down the gauntlet. "Maybe if Josh holds your hand, you'll cross the street."

Toby sneered and I thought he was going to rush

Rishi, but then again Rishi was standing next to old Fists of Fury himself: me. Instead, Toby walked right up to the house, stopped in front of one of the stone lions, and planted a big kiss on it. Some kids shouted approval while others laughed. Toby just strutted back from the house, high-fived Josh, and turned to us. "Now, can any of you top that one?"

"Ooooh. Kissing a lion. Like that's supposed to mean something?" Rishi countered. "The lion is at the end of the walkway. You didn't even make it onto the porch. Do something brave, then start talking."

At this Josh walked toward Rishi and the air grew colder. He glanced down at him and I thought I could see the faint outline of a mustache growing above his lip in the moonlight. Josh walked away from us past Toby and right on up to the Johnson porch. Reaching the front door, he pulled his leg back and kicked. I could clearly hear the loud thud. Satisfied that he had caused enough damage, he shuffled back to us.

Toby smiled at Josh, and the two of them turned and faced the crowd. Toby said, "There, big mouth. No one's done that before, and I know none of you will even come close." The crowd started clapping and I almost joined in. Toby was right, though. No one was topping that.

Rishi held up his left hand to silence the crowd. His right hand gripped my shoulder. He began, "Not bad but, come on, I thought we all came down here to see something impressive."

Knowing what was coming, I tried to interrupt. "Uh . . ."

"Relax, buddy, I know you're eager to start." And then to Toby and Josh, "What, you think Rodney here is afraid of this place?"

Heck yes! Please shut up.

But he didn't. "Most of you saw what he did to the McThuggs. Rodney can handle those stone lions. He could easily kiss them, tickle them, or ride them home if he wanted to. . . ."

I tried to interrupt again. "Um, I haven't studied for that science test yet, so . . ."

"It's okay, pal," Rishi continued. "I know you want to get to it."

No, idiot!

He turned and looked right at Toby. "He can do anything you can do." Then, looking at Josh, Rishi continued, "Or you, and a lot more!"

"*Any*thing?" Toby asked. I wanted to grab Rishi and throttle him, but before I could . . .

"Yeah, *any*thing," he said, poking his finger into Toby's chest.

Toby looked down at the finger for a moment and then looked up at me. With sparkling eyes that reflected the large moon, he said, "I bet he won't go *in* the house."

This brought on a round of gasps. The kids gradually stopped talking and all looked at me, waiting for a response. I did the only thing I could do—scramble for an excuse.

"Hey, that sounds like it would be something." I took a deep breath and continued, "There's nothing I'd rather do, but you see, there's a problem. The house is going to be locked. I mean . . ."

My logical, convincing point was interrupted. Not by Toby, Josh, or Rishi. Not by any other kid standing there, but by the front door of Old Man Johnson's house. For the first time that night, it creaked slightly open in the breeze. Two kids immediately bolted off down the street. I would have joined them, but Rishi's hand was still gripping my shoulder, now much tighter, and I couldn't move.

Jaws dropped as all of us stood staring at the door. It slowly blew closed again. Once he got his voice back, Toby said, "There. That solves that problem."

For the first time in weeks, Josh looked directly at me. Everything had stopped. I could feel his eyes piercing me, and I knew that all the gains I had made since the first day of school would be lost that night if I didn't go into the house. And shockingly, even though my heart and brain both screamed no, my foot took a step forward. Then another. I reached for the gate.

The stone lions seemed to be looking at me, glaring. I shuddered, exhaled and continued very slowly up the broken steps. It was much darker up here by the house. "Go for it, Rodney!" I heard Rishi shout.

There had to be some way out of this. *Just jump in for a second*, I told myself. Wait. What was I thinking? Not a chance. *Okay, Plan B. Turn and run and never return to Garrettsville.* I had made it to the porch and was shaking uncontrollably when the front door suddenly creaked open.

"Pssst. Hey kid."

I almost wet my pants. Someone was right there. I could see a white hand holding the doorknob.

"Relax. Come here."

I focused on the sound and could see in the shadows what looked like an old man in pajamas and a robe. His face lit up and I noticed he was smoking a pipe.

"That's right, I'm not going to eat you. I've been listening to your rather amusing discussion, and if you do want to come in, I promise not to chop your head off." That sent a shudder down my spine. "Oh, sorry, just some Halloween humor." He laughed. His laugh wasn't menacing, and he seemed old and not very threatening. I weighed my options. Realizing I'd rather face this guy than a year of Josh's poundings, I stepped in.

There was a faint light coming from the living room and a fire in the fireplace. It seemed almost cozy, not the bloodstained torture chamber I expected. "Well, my dear boy, now that you're here, have a seat." He motioned to one of two big armchairs near the fire.

"Uh, thank you," I said.

"You're certainly very welcome. But I must say you

are the first to actually enter my family home, and I'm not really prepared for it." He took a puff on his pipe and the smoke smelled sweet and smooth. "Care to join me in a drink? Oh wait, I guess you're more of a milk drinker at your age. I have some club soda. That's the best I can do, I'm afraid." He brought a tray from the kitchen and poured the drinks. I tried to control my breathing. I had calmed down some, but the scene was still creepy. "I see you're not going to be saying much, so I'll start. I'm Old Man Johnson. At least I am this year. And you are?"

"Rodney, sir."

"Well, Rodney, sadly I didn't murder anyone and I'm not possessed by the devil."

"So why does everyone think . . ."

"That this place is haunted? Well, laddy, they do so because my brother wants them to. He lives here and loves a good fright. In actuality, I'm a Broadway actor who grew up in this house but moved away years ago. My brother is traveling and asked if I would take over the honors this Halloween. I'm between shows and jumped at the chance." He turned slightly and glanced around the room. "Not exactly the Hamptons, but it's home. And now you have discovered my secret. I never expected anyone would actually try to enter the house. You must be very brave."

"Not really," I admitted. As my eyes became adjusted to the light, I jumped after noticing a human skull sitting on the coffee table. I cleared my throat. "Actually, I'm a big chicken." I was shocked I had said it out loud, but it felt good to talk about it.

"How interesting. So how did a coward find the nerve to enter the front door?"

"Well, I had to, to keep my tough guy reputation."

"And how did you get that?" Before I knew it, I was telling him all the stuff that had happened to me. He seemed interested and asked, "Rodney, why is this reputation so important to you? Not every kid has one, and what you go through to keep yours seems more trouble than it's . . ."

"That's where you're wrong. This year's been a dream. In my last school, back in New York there was this kid Rocco . . ."

"New York? Did you say New York? Surely you saw me play Macbeth at the Orpheum Theater?"

"Uh, no. But anyway, last year this bully, Rocco, would beat me up almost every day. Whenever I was on line, he would cut in front of me. I lived each day scared of his fists and atomic wedgies. I don't want to ever go back to that. And just as important, there's this girl in my class, Jessica, who I want to impress."

"I see. Well, Rodney, we have an interesting situation. We both have a secret, and we both want it kept. Besides, for you, the only person in this town who knows I'm here is my brother. If I help you with your secret, will you keep mine?"

"Absolutely," I answered.

"Splendid! I assume that motley crew of boys outside is with you?"

"Some are; some I wish weren't."

"Oh, are Josh and Toby out there?" he asked. He knew them from my story.

"Yeah," I answered.

"And is your young lassie out there?"

I thought he was talking about a dog until I realized he meant Jessica. I shook my head no.

"Well then, she'll miss all the fun. You see, you've already been in here for over ten minutes, so by now everyone out there must think you're dead, or worse!" I wasn't sure what was worse than death but I let him continue. "Since you know of my acting ability, you'll be happy to hear I've decided to stage a final scene to really put them over the top. I plan to screech like when I played Gloucester in *King Lear*. The critics loved my take on that role."

He went over to the window. "Come. Watch your friends." I peeked out through the shutter and the next thing I knew, Old Man Johnson was shouting, "No! Noooooooooo, Rodney!!! I'm sorry I crossed you! AAArrrrrggggggggghhhhhhhhh!!!!!!!!" Sure enough they all bolted in every direction.

My new friend laughed. "That ought to help you a bit. I'll let out one final scream once you're on the porch, just to silence the cynics in the crowd who might believe you gave a one-man performance in here." He sure talked funny, but I liked him a lot. We shook hands and he said, "Thank you, my boy, for a most pleasant Halloween." Then he noticed me staring at the skull. "You like Philip?"

"Uhh . . ."

"Don't get jumpy. I just call him that. I use him to practice Hamlet, but he comes in handy on Halloween, too. Why don't you take him as a little trick-or-treat present?"

"All right, thanks, I guess." I picked up Philip, tucked him in my jacket, waved good-bye to Mr. Johnson, and stepped out onto the porch. True to his word, he let out one final moan from inside the house that could be heard a mile away.

When I reached the street I didn't see anyone at first, but then I noticed some boys hiding in the bushes. When they saw me they started to emerge like ants out of holes. They gathered around, shocked to see me alive. After a bit, their fear and shock wore off and more of the original crowd began to join us. They cheered and everyone kept asking me questions. I just said it was no big deal and started walking home.

"Come on, Rodney! What the heck happened in there?" Rishi asked.

"Go in there yourself if you want to find out," I replied. I knew that would silence him. I was still a little annoyed at how he had egged on Josh and Toby, who now stood gaping at me a few feet away. I smiled at them. "Nice idea, Toby, daring me to go inside the house. Oh, I got you guys a souvenir." With that I took out Philip and tossed it to them.

Josh caught it, unaware of what it was, but when he saw a smiling human skull looking up at him, he wailed, "Whoooooooahhhhh!" just as Rishi took his picture.

The next day was yet another one of stories and tales. Some of the stories had me wrestling the ghost of Old Man Johnson. Others pinned me against escaped prisoners hiding out in the house. In all the tales I was heroic, and I never corrected anyone.

At one point before lunch Jessica came up to me. "You're full of surprises, Rodney Rathbone," she smiled. "I'm not sure what to make of you." My face blushed and before I could figure out an answer she walked off to join Kayla.

The only person not celebrating that day was a quiet, angry Toby sitting in the row next to me. I ignored him, but I should have given him more thought. I was soon to learn that each of my victories—and his embarrassing defeats—only made him more determined to see me fail.

Chapter 9

THE INVINCIBLE BOY

The weeks following Halloween were free and easy, with the possible exception of the day Toby tried to get me kicked out of school. Honestly, it was one of the dumbest things I've ever seen . . . even for Toby.

After I emerged from Old Man Johnson's house unharmed, my reputation had only grown. Walking down the halls in school had actually started to tire me out. Not one kid passed without a "Hey Rodney," or "Hi, Rodney" or "How's it going, Rodney?" At night my hand hurt from high-fiving everyone. Sometimes it got so crazy at school that Rishi had to step in.

"Mr. Rathbone can't play ball with you today at recess because he already promised Frank and James a game of hoops. I'll check his schedule and get back to you. Maybe next week." He said he was my agent.

It seemed the more popular I got, the more I noticed Toby whispering in Josh's ear. It didn't take a genius to know they were plotting something. After all, their whole world had been turned upside down. If they tried to pick on a kid this year, Dave or Slim would say, "I wouldn't do that if I was you" and motion in my direction. I just played it cool and let my reputation do the talking.

The afternoon before we left for the long Thanksgiving weekend is when Toby made his move. I was coming back from the boys' room in the middle of class when I turned the corner and saw him and Josh standing in front of me, Josh making a fist and rubbing it with his left hand. The hall was empty. It all happened so fast that I didn't even have time to panic. I just remember my brain saying, *This is it.* Josh pulled back his right arm as far as he could and sent it flying forward. I braced and heard the punch connect—pow!—right into Toby's face.

What happened next shocked me even more. Toby screamed, "Rodney punched me!!! Help! My nose is bleeding! Somebody, Rodney punched me and called me names!" Trying to get away before a teacher came out of class, Josh ran smack into Mr. Feebletop, who had turned the corner in time to see the whole show.

"Nice try, you half-wits," he muttered to Josh and Toby. "Let's take a little walk to my office." Then he turned to me. "Only eighty-four more days till spring training!" I just nodded.

As they disappeared down the hall, I heard Toby tell Josh, "Stop smiling, you jerk. That really hurt."

Of course, everyone within earshot of Toby's shouts thought I had finally decked him for good. That day, two hundred kids must have come up to me and said, "He had it coming. You rule!"

I would just shrug each time, look bored, and mumble, "I guess."

On the bus ride home, Josh and Toby glared out the window as Rishi tortured them. "First we got you, Josh, with one punch to the nose. Then we decided it was your turn, Toby. . . ." I wasn't sure who this "we" was, but Rishi seemed happy so I kept quiet. Every once in a while Toby would spin around, start to say something, change his mind, and give me a long hard stare. He knew and I knew that he would never tell anyone what really had happened in the hallway—and it was sure driving him nuts.

Sitting there, full, after a great Thanksgiving dinner, watching football with my dad, I remember thinking that I was perhaps invincible. And for the next month it felt that way. Despite Mrs. Lutzkraut doing her best Ebenezer Scrooge imitation, December slid happily along. In fact, I had to eat lunch with her only twice. Josh and Toby were keeping their distance, and the best part was Jessica. Lately she had started talking to me more and more. Even Kayla had begun to act halfway nice, though one day before Christmas vacation I found out why.

"You know," Jessica whispered to me on the way back from art class, "Kayla likes Dave." I almost fainted . . . not from the news but the smell of Jessica's long blond hair so close to my face. It smelled like strawberries and vanilla.

"Are you listening to me?" she asked.

"Um, yeah," I answered, fumbling with some books in my hand. "How do you know Kayla likes him?"

"Duh, Rathbone. She *told* me."

It was the first time I liked listening to my last name. It sounded great coming from her lips. *Stay focused!* "Well, Jessica, I don't know if *he* likes her."

"But maybe you could do something or say something to him over the break. You seem to be able to do anything." Then she reached out, held my wrist gently in her hand, and looked into my eyes. "Couldn't you do it as a special favor for me?"

Thump. Thump. Thump.

"Rodney?"

Thump. Thump. Thump. Thump . . .

"Are you okay, Rodney?"

"Jessica, I was wondering if sometime you might . . ."

"Am I interrupting?" Rishi interrupted. I felt Jessica's hand let go, and she ran off to catch up with her friends. For once, though, I was kind of glad Rishi had a big mouth. I was still afraid that if I asked Jessica out, she might say no. I needed a few more weeks to get up my nerve.

Right before heading to bed that night, content that everything was going better than I could possibly dream, I glanced out the window and noticed that it had started to snow. "Hey, check it out!" I yelled to my parents.

"Ooooohhh it's snowing," my mom exclaimed. "The weatherman didn't say anything about . . ."

She was interrupted by my dad, who sang in her ear, "'I'm dreaming of a white Christmas, just like the ones . . .'"

"You are no Bing Crosby," she giggled back, grabbing him. I watched the two of them goofing around. The fire crackled. My sister was in bed. Christmas was only two days away. Everything was perfect. I returned to looking outside and smiled at the falling snow. It wasn't long before I'd be cursing every flake.

Chapter 10

I MEET THE BEAST

Early Christmas morning my sister woke me up and we tore down the steps to the living room where my parents waited, surrounded by presents. My sister squealed with delight as she opened little packages containing Polly Pockets or Barbies, but I looked intently for the one gift I wanted. I shredded green and red paper, made mincemeat of bows, and dumped the clothes, books, and other things to the side. Once I finished opening everything, I sat back, quiet, trying to hide my disappointment.

"Rodney, you didn't look under the chair," my dad said. I zoomed around, and there it was, badly wrapped, indicating my father had done it—a box that was just the right size.

I started ripping it open and he jumped up to join me. My mom said, "Donald, is that what I think it is? How much was it?" My dad just laughed and grabbed me and we tore into the den to set up the most advanced video-game system around.

While it might have been my present, I think my dad had bought it for himself. The two of us played video games for the next few days as the snow fell softly outside. Then one morning my mom walked in and pulled the plug on us right in the middle of a tennis match. We stood looking at her in shock.

"Donald, do you really want to spend your few days off this Christmas playing video games? Don't you think you should finish cleaning out the basement?" My mom's questions weren't questions; they were orders. "And you," she said, turning to me now, "don't you want to go outside and play in the snow?"

Don't you want to leave me alone? I almost blurted out, but this was my mom and even I knew better.

She continued, "I have to clean the house. We're having the Windbaggers over for dinner."

"Aaaaaggghhhhhh!" My dad and I whined simultaneously.

"Now, now," she continued. "We're new to this town, Donald. Fred and Ethel were good enough to have you and me over last month." My dad let out a sigh. I hadn't met them yet, but my dad groaned every time he heard their name.

"And anyway, Rodney . . ." Somehow I knew what was coming and my stomach tightened. ". . . Don't you want to go sledding with your friends?"

Ever since the snow started falling I knew one of my

parents would bring up sledding. I hated sledding. The way other kids hate going to the dentist, that's how I feel about going to the top of some hill and zooming down a million miles an hour. My dad is a big sled and toboggan guy and had taken me years ago, but I screamed and cried the whole way down the hill. We hadn't returned.

"I don't know, Mom. Don't you need help cleaning or something?"

She looked at me like I had two heads and was about to open her mouth when the doorbell rang. "Probably one of the neighbors," she said, slightly annoyed.

I followed her to the door, adding, "And besides, none of my new friends in Garrettsville are into sledding."

Upon opening the door we were greeted by Rishi, standing there holding a sled.

"Hey Rodney! We're going to the Hill. Do you want to come up there with us?" he asked.

Before I could even make up some lie about chores, my mom answered for me. "Yes, he does, Rishi. Isn't that right, Rodney?"

"Great!" Rishi shouted and came in while my mom dug out my snow clothes. The fear began pumping through my veins. I had to get out of this. Thoughts of me shooting down a large hill and crashing and busting my head open went through my mind. Even worse, what if I panicked at the top of the hill and the kids made fun of me? This would be another day of having to maintain my toughness and bravery and lies. I could feel the hand of doom reaching out and patting me on the shoulder. Actually it was Rishi.

"We can share my sled," he suggested.

For a second I relaxed. At least with someone else to steer, I could close my eyes and hope for the best. And more important, none of the kids would discover that the great Rodney Rathbone knew nothing about turning or stopping a sled.

"Nonsense!" my father shouted as he walked up the basement steps. "I have the best sled in the world for you."

"Cool, Mr. Rathbone," Rishi answered.

Way to go, Dad. Why don't you just push me off a cliff?

"Come on!" My dad led us outside. We had to run to keep up with him. Finding his ladder in the junk-filled garage, he told me to hold the bottom as he climbed the rickety steps to the storage area above. After some groans and muttering, he started to slide a long orange plastic sled down to the floor. It must have been at least six feet long. He got it down, grabbed it, and held it up for us to examine. "This, boys, is the Beast. It is the fastest, best sled I've ever owned, and now it's yours."

"Wow! That's awesome," Rishi exclaimed. "You'll be the king of the Hill! Won't you, Rodney?"

"No question about it!" my dad shouted back.

"Uh, great," I muttered, but my dad and his favorite new son were too excited to notice my lack of enthusiasm.

"There is no sled that can match it," my dad continued.

"Excellent! You're going to travel at light speed, Rodney."

"Swell." I gulped.

Possibly sensing my hesitation, my dad added, "Don't worry. It's easy to steer. If you want to turn to the right, just drag your right hand a little in the snow. That will create some drag and turn you in that direction. It's a cinch, and like I said, this sled is the best. Now get out there on that hill." He closed the garage and bounded up the steps into the house. I watched him go, wishing I could share some of his excitement, not to mention his skill with a sled. With a downcast, worried heart, I headed off with Rishi to the Hill.

Chapter 11

KING OF THE HILL

After thirty minutes' trudging along with a six-foot sled and a fool for a friend, I was tired and in no better mood.

"You're going to love the Hill. It's huge. Look, there it is."

He wasn't lying. It was gigantic and, despite it being cold out, sweat dripped down my body beneath my layers. I stood for a moment at the bottom, taking it all in. Hundreds of people young and old were sledding in every direction, some down wide-open runs, others down narrow trails through wooded areas. I was about to stick my head into a snowdrift when my friends spotted me.

"Hey, Rodney's here!" Dave yelled.

"Rodney's here. Now the day can really start," Slim added. They all walked up, admiring my sled. Other kids from school came running up to greet me.

"I'm here, t-too," Rishi stammered.

Ignoring Rishi, Slim observed, "Wow, that's some sled, Rodney. It's huge. I bet it's fast."

"Yeah," I agreed.

"Then you better know everything about the Hill, because some of the trails are superdangerous."

"Yeah, especially the Slaughter House Trail," Rishi added.

"Slaughter House?" I gulped. I hoped I didn't sound as scared as I felt.

"Yeah, no one goes down that anymore. The last person to try it was Dave's cousin, and he broke his leg."

"He hit a tree," Dave explained.

Slim continued, "Yeah, he had to turn into the tree, otherwise he would have fallen into the Ravine of Doom—and then you're a goner. But we don't sled anywhere near it."

My relief was short-lived. "Yeah, 'cause you're *too scared*!" Toby's unmistakable voice sounded behind us. "Josh and I just got off the Wild Thing and didn't see you girls over there. Did you see them, Josh?"

Josh stood behind Toby wearing his leather jacket and smirking. "Nope," he answered. It was the most I had heard out of him since Thanksgiving.

Toby dropped his sled and began squeezing a snowball, making it hard and round till it turned to ice. He looked up at me, and for a fleeting second I saw he wanted to throw it right at my face. Instead he turned and launched it at some kindergartners. It landed several feet in front of a little kid in a Spider-Man hat. Toby frowned.

"Nice throw." Rishi laughed. Toby sneered but I saw him notice the Beast, and maybe its size and bright orange plastic sheen silenced him.

"You like it?" Rishi asked him. "If you're real polite, maybe Rodney won't flatten you with it."

With that, we left our snarling foes and followed Rishi up the Hill. I realized that by the time the day was over, there was a very good chance I would either break a leg or pee in my pants. Neither option appealed to me.

We kept going. The higher we went, the steeper it got. At one point, Slim, never graceful, slipped and slid all the way down on his back.

"Real nice," a girl's voice shouted from close behind us. "You look like a big upside-down turtle!" The voice was very familiar, so I wasn't surprised when I turned and saw Kayla laughing. She wasn't alone. Samantha stood in a white coat, also laughing at Slim, and beyond her, in a pink outfit, stood Jessica. Instead of feeling happy, I couldn't believe my bad luck. The last thing I needed was her seeing me wipe out! Swallowing the fear bubbling up inside me, I followed Dave and Rishi to the top.

Far below us, you could see all the streets and parks of Garrettsville and I could even see Baber Intermediate in the distance, but up here it was quiet. The wind seemed to blow all other sound away. Rishi looked over at Dave and me and said, "Okay, let's do it."

"Wait, the girls are in our way," Dave pointed out. "They'll be up to us in a minute."

We stood, shivering, as they approached. The sky had turned dark gray and snow had started to fall. Suddenly I wished I had never pretended to be anything other than what I really am—a coward. I wouldn't have to keep proving myself to everyone. I wouldn't be standing up here terrified at what was about to happen. I could be at home in my cozy room. . . .

"What's with him?" I heard Kayla ask. I looked up and noticed everyone staring at me. "You look like you're about to cry."

"No way," I said. "I was just trying to figure out the scariest, craziest way to head down this molehill."

"Molehill?" Rishi shouted. "Did you hear him? My man Rodney's not afraid of ANYthing!"

I looked at Jessica and the two of us smiled. In an instant I knew I'd rather crash than admit I was chicken in front of her or my friends.

"That's a pretty nice sled," she said, pointing to the Beast.

"Uh, yeah, well, it's . . ."

"What he means to say," Rishi interjected, "is would you like to ride with him on it?"

"Well, I don't know, it looks pretty fast. . . ."

"Oh, it *is* fast, Jessica, but it's nothing Rodney can't handle. He was like the sledding champion of New York."

Shut up, you imbecile.

Then he turned toward me and whispered, "It's time you thought about giving your agent a raise. I'm working overtime here. Go have fun, buddy."

"Okay, I'll go with you, Rodney," Jessica agreed, smiling a little nervously.

Terrific, now when I mess up I'll be taking her with me. I wondered if she'd still talk to me after we smashed into a tree. I gulped again and climbed into the sled in back of Jessica. Her hair blew into my face and—lost up there, on top of the hill in the clouds—I thought I was in heaven. Until Kayla's voice brought me back to earth.

"My sled! My sled slid down the mountain! Isn't anyone going to do anything?" The girls had brought only two sleds with them in the first place, and now Kayla had conveniently set one free. "Dave," she began, "I have an idea. Maybe I could ride down with you on *your* sled." You had to give her credit.

"Uh, sure, Kayla. Hop on."

"Well, now that we're all set," Rishi announced, "let's do this."

Dave and Kayla were the first ones to head down. As they shoved off, I thought I heard Kayla tell Dave, "Hold me tighter!" Samantha followed, and then Rishi pushed off. As Jessica and I adjusted ourselves, the Beast started moving forward on its own.

"Rodney, promise me that you won't do anything

crazy," Jessica yelled back as we suddenly shot down the frighteningly steep slope. I was too petrified to answer. "Rodney?" she shouted. Sitting in front of me, Jessica couldn't see the panic on my face. My dad wasn't kidding when he said I'd have the fastest sled on the hill. We were zooming down the trail and already coming up on the other guys. I heard Rishi shout, "Way to go!"

The first big turn was coming. I tried frantically to remember what my dad had said about steering. Wanting to turn right, I pushed down hard with my left hand. The Beast immediately swung farther to the left and, before I had time to think, we were zipping between two bushes straight onto Slaughter House Trail. We passed right in front of a shocked Toby and Josh, and in the corner of my eye I saw their sleds smash into each other.

"Slow down, Rodney!" Jessica was shrieking. "You promised me . . ."

It was Rishi's voice ringing out behind us that brought me back to my senses. He yelled, "Rodney's heading for the Ravine of Doom!" The Beast was now traveling at warp speed and seemed to have a mind of its own.

"Are you sure you know what you're doing?" Jessica screamed, clutching onto my legs. She didn't exactly sound happy and I was way too terrified to answer. My brain completely shut down. I didn't know what was coming, and even if I did, I couldn't do anything about it.

The Beast was in its glory. We were an orange blur and

just about airborne when I heard Rishi shout, "Watch out for the Ravine of Doom!"

"Ahhhhhhhhhhhhhhhhhhhhhhhh!!!" Jessica screamed as we flew straight off the cliff. The Beast sailed above boulders, and I could see little kids far below at the bottom of the Hill staring up at us. Jessica continued screaming and had turned and buried her face in my chest. Her eyes were closed and she couldn't see the fear in my own eyes. *We're dead, we're dead, we're dead*, was all I could think.

We started to plunge. I clapped my eyes shut. The Beast bounced off something hard that slowed us but we almost flipped and did two complete circles before coming to a gradual stop in the midst of a crowd at the bottom of the Hill. I later found out the "something hard" we hit was a giant igloo some kids had spent the morning building. Poor kids.

"It's okay," I managed to squeak. Jessica was silent and I realized she was probably crying. We may have survived, but I was sure our friendship hadn't. I braced for the worst. She tentatively let go of me and looked up at the crowd gathering around us. Then it happened. She flashed a great big smile and said, "That was amazing! You're crazy! How did you do that? No one's ever gone off the Ravine of Doom. You made it seem so easy!"

I exhaled and looked up toward the heavens. Somehow I had done it again. "Ah, well, us New York sledding champions, we've got a few moves, you know. . . ."

"Rodney, that was the coolest thing any boy in this town has ever done," she explained as she stood up. By now my gang and half the population of Garrettsville had made it over to us. They all seemed to be saying the same thing, that it was the greatest sledding feat in the history of the Hill.

Disheveled, covered in snow, and not looking too happy, Josh and Toby came wandering up. Toby turned to Josh and said, "Who does this guy think he is, Evel Knievel?" Josh didn't answer. He was looking down at the front of his beloved leather jacket. It was ripped from top to bottom, undoubtedly torn in the crash. The crash I had caused. His eyes slowly looked up at mine. They were deadly serious. Not since the first day of school had he given me such a threatening look. He held my gaze for a number of slow seconds, grabbed his sled, and walked off. Toby looked one last time at me and the cheering crowd, shook his head in disbelief, grabbed his sled, and followed Josh.

The snow had stopped and the sun was actually shining brightly. We decided to stay at the Hill for a while longer and spent time over on the Bunny Bouncer, where I gave rides to all the little kids who wanted to experience the now legendary Beast. Jessica told them what it was like and how I had steered like a master.

After a couple of hours and a warm good-bye from her, I was walking home, lugging the Beast and smiling to myself, when I heard a hey come from a bush.

"Huh?" I mumbled, looking at it.

Dave's head popped up. He looked from side to side. "Is the coast clear?"

I laughed. Kayla was nowhere in sight. "Yeah, it's clear."

"Thanks, Rodney," and with that he was off and running.

A few blocks from home, while wondering what my mom had made for dinner, I heard the loud, unmistakable rumble of a motorcycle roar from behind me. Oh no, how could I have forgotten? The McThuggs were bound to come for revenge at some point. I gulped and glanced back.

Sitting there on a huge bike was a mean-looking guy. "You Rodney Ratbone?" he growled. I wasn't about to correct him about my last name. For a second I debated whether to drop the Beast and make a run for it, but eventually I just nodded my head. The guy continued, "I'm T-Bone, T-Bone Ratfield. I just wanted to thank you for taking care of J. D. McThugg and his brothers. Going in there with a rat shirt and attacking them with bees, now that's brilliant. Hop on. I'll give you and your sled a ride home."

"Uh, I'm almost there," I answered, remembering my lessons about strangers.

"All right then, but you're now an honorary Ratfield, Ratbone. Ha-ha. *Ratbone* got *rat* in it, just like *Ratfield*. We're probably related." He got off the bike and came up to me. "Since we is family and all, I'm going to teach you the Ratfield secret handshake." We worked through a bizarre set of moves. Once I got it down, he gave me a friendly whack on the back and rode off into the winter sunset.

Chapter 12

DINNER WITH THE WINDBAGGERS

I left the Beast in the front yard and walked into the house. My dad, seated in his chair in the living room by the fire, greeted me with a smile. "How was sledding? That's some sled, right?"

"Dad, you have no idea." He didn't say anything, but he turned his gaze toward the fire. A twinkle in his eye told me that maybe he did.

The twinkle in his eye was extinguished when my mother called, "Donald, did you finish setting the table? The Windbaggers will be here any minute."

I had never met the Windbaggers but somehow knew that I wouldn't like them. Maybe it was because of the face my father made whenever my mother mentioned their name. It was a face like he was sucking on a lemon.

Moments later the doorbell rang. "Rodney, will you let them in?" my mom called from the kitchen. Penny beat me to it and opened the door. The Windbaggers rushed in along with an arctic chill.

"Cold out there!" Mr. Windbagger boomed, stomping the snow from his shoes on the mat.

"Oh, aren't you precious?" Mrs. Windbagger said, patting Penny on the head. "What's your name?"

"Penny."

"Fred, isn't she just adorable?"

"Gotta love a kid named after money," Mr. Windbagger said. "And you must be Rodney? Heard a lot about you." He stuck out his hand. I reached out and shook it. "No, no!" he said. "Your hand feels like a dead fish. Put some muscle into it." I squeezed hard and jerked my arm up and down. "That's it. When you're in the business world, Rodney, a good handshake lets the other guy know who's boss."

Mr. Windbagger let go of my hand and turned to my dad, who had entered the hall and caught the end of the handshaking lesson. "Donald, good to see you."

"You too, Fred." My dad had that lemon face on.

Next thing I knew, their hands met with a thunderous clap. I watched their fingers tighten and their grins harden. I didn't know if they were shaking hands or arm wrestling. Mr. Windbagger's head turned red and a vein on my dad's forearm began to bulge.

"Okay, you two, stop horsing around," my mom said. "Let's go have some appetizers by the fire. Donald, fix the drinks. Rodney, take the coats." My dad and I attended to our assigned tasks, and fortunately, unlike my father, I was able to sneak off to the den to play video games.

Before I logged on to the game, I checked my e-mail. There was a message waiting for me from Timmy. It read,

> Rodney, I have the best news! While he was choking me, Rocco mentioned that he might be moving! Isn't that great?

I smiled as I wrote back congratulating him. Maybe things really do work out for the best. Grinning, I clicked off the computer and clicked on the game console. I had just blasted my fifth Nazi when my dad appeared next to me on the couch.

"This two-player?"

"It can be," I told him. My dad picked up the other controller and joined in. Together we blew up a machine-gun nest and a tank.

Penny, who always seemed to sense when I was having fun, came in and announced, "Mom says you need to wash up for dinner." She then added, "Dad, what are you doing? You're supposed to be with the Windbaggers. Mom wouldn't like it if she knew . . ."

"I was just fixing a draft." Dropping the controller, he sprinted back to the living room as I headed for the bathroom. After rinsing my hands, I sat down at my seat at the dining room table before the adults entered.

The heavy steps of Mr. Windbagger banged down

the wood floor in the hall. He walked in and planted himself in my dad's seat at the head of the table. As my dad entered behind him, I could see his eyes narrow. He looked like he was about to resume shaking hands. Before he could start anything with Windbagger, though, my mom suggested, "Donald, why don't you sit between Penny and me down here?"

Mr. Windbagger's mouth immediately started blabbing. "What's for dinner? I'm starved."

"Spaghetti," my mom answered.

"You New Yorkers and your fancy foreign foods." He shook his head and laughed, shoved some pasta into his mouth, and went right on talking. "I got one heck of a deal on a new Cadillac. Rodney, after dinner I'll take you for a ride. It's got heated seats."

"Wonderful," I said. My mom caught my sarcasm and flashed me a look.

Suddenly Mr. Windbagger swung his leg up on the table, almost toppling my glass of milk. He pulled his pant leg up to his knee, and I looked at his fleshy, hairy calf. The spaghetti lost some appeal. "You see these socks, Rodney? They're silk. Cost more than this table." He rapped his knuckles on the oak. "Do you know what that says to people?"

That you're nuts, I thought.

"It says this guy's a success. People say, 'That's the guy I want handling my money.'"

I noticed my dad refill his wineglass.

My mom cut in. "Donald and I are so glad you could join us for dinner. . . . Right, Donald . . . *Donald*?"

"Absolutely." He choked.

My mom went on. "With most of our friends and family living back east, it's nice to have an evening like this, with new friends. And speaking of our friends back in New York, I have a little announcement I wanted to share with my kids."

Mrs. Windbagger smiled kindly at Penny and me.

My mom continued, "I was talking to my friend Michelle, back in Bayside, about how nice it is here. Her husband, Vinny, works from home. He can basically live and work anywhere, and they don't need to be paying New York's high prices." I didn't know what this had to do with me, but at least it shut up Mr. Windbagger for a moment. "Anyway, they've decided to visit Ohio, to see if they like it, and if they do, they're going to move here. If everything goes according to schedule, they'll be here before the spring. Isn't that great news?"

"Who's Michelle and Vinny again?" I asked.

"Rodney, *you* know. The *Ronbonis*. Rocco's parents."

I choked on a meatball. Penny turned to me. "As in Rocco Ronboni!"

I thought about the e-mail I had just read from Timmy. Rocco was moving, all right. He was moving here! It was now only a matter of time. I could almost hear my last minutes ticking down like a clock inside my head. My nice little run was over.

Chapter 13

A TIGHTS SQUEEZE

For the remainder of the holiday break I was a nervous wreck. Rocco Ronboni was heading west. I didn't know when, and it might be over a month away, but he was coming. It was like an approaching storm I couldn't stop. He knew who I *really* was. When he got here, he'd go right back to beating me up. Of course, as soon as he did, Josh and Toby would join in. Then, seeing what a true wimp I am, other kids would want to get in on the fun. My life would be full of bruises and pain. I imagined that my friends wouldn't want to hang out with the big phony named Rodney Rathbone. And any chance of landing a cute blond girlfriend would be lost for good.

I pleaded with my mom to tell them not to come, but she merely said, "Don't be silly, Rodney. You always played so nicely together when you were younger. Remember when you used to play Marco Polo at the public pool?"

"Yeah, I remember. Every time he caught me, he held my head underwater."

"What an imagination you have. . . ."

"Mom, I still have water in my left ear!"

"Rodney, you're going to be late for school. Just think, you'll be able to introduce Rocco to everyone."

She was so excited to have one of her friends from the old neighborhood coming to visit that she couldn't listen to sense.

I decided to try my dad. "Can't you speak to mom for me?" I pleaded.

He took a deep breath and answered, "Rodney, one day when you're married you'll realize wives rarely listen to their husbands. I'm afraid we're stuck with your mother's choice in friends. You get this creepy Rocco and I get Fred Windbagger."

"But Fred Windbagger doesn't give you wedgies. . . ."

"You might prefer a wedgie to a two-hour life insurance conversation."

"Dad . . ."

"Rodney, you've handled some tough characters this year. I've been proud of you, and I'm sure this Rocco's going to meet his match too."

Now it's nice to have a dad who's proud of you, but I wondered how proud he'd be after I got pounded to a pulp by half the town. The only good news was that Rocco and his family wouldn't be here for a while.

• • •

As I walked into school the first day back, I realized the other kids didn't know about my private problems. All they could talk about was my flight off the Ravine of Doom. And it wasn't just because they had seen it in person. A father who had been there filming his five-year-old twins had heard some shouts, had turned his camera in my direction, and had captured most of my amazing trip on video. A week later it had made its way to YouTube and was now one of the most popular videos.

Yes, that January my celebrity status was at an all-time high, and while it did wonders to help me forget about Rocco, it didn't do much to impress the one person I hoped it would: Jessica. As I tried to talk to her I could see that she was okay with me, but it felt like her mind was on something, or someone, else.

Maybe it was just the time of year. The dreariness of winter had settled in on us. The weather was bad and we were stuck inside during recess. To make matters worse, each time my big mouth got me in trouble I would have to spend recess alone with Mrs. Lutzkraut, watching her eat disgusting squishy sandwiches and slurpy soups, all followed by her one treat—chocolates. The woman loved chocolate. The first time I saw her eat any I thought she was fainting. She swooned, kind of shook for a second, smiled, and closed her eyes. As soon as the chocolates were gone, her face would regain the nasty look I'd come to know and despise.

There was nothing pleasant about Mrs. Lutzkraut or

her drab classroom. It became darker and sadder with each cold January day. It was during one particularly long, depressing afternoon that she surprised us.

"I've decided to put on a play this year." We all sat up. "You know, I was quite the actress in my younger years."

"Yeah, bet she was a great Medusa," I whispered to Rishi.

She turned in our direction. Rishi and I stared straight ahead. It was Samantha who broke the silence.

"Are we doing *High School Musical*?"

Mrs. Lutzkraut took a deep breath. "No, Samantha. We are doing a *real* play. We will be putting on *Robin Hood*." The class broke into a discussion and Mrs. Lutzkraut glared us back into silence. "Now, if I may continue, I've already decided on the parts."

Jessica, not surprisingly, would be our Maid Marion. Kayla would be an evil witch, which also made sense to me. Rishi was cast as the sheriff of Nottingham, one of the villains. Dave got the part of Will Scarlet, one of the Merry Men. Toby was told he would be Friar Tuck. He sat there scowling, but he was always scowling and I couldn't tell from his reaction whether he liked his role or not.

"What about me?" Slim asked excitedly. "Do I get a part?"

"I have decided to give you the part of Little John."

"But Mrs. Lutzkraut, I'm not little," Slim observed.

"Precisely, Timothy. It's called irony. It's much funnier

to have the part of Little John played by someone big and plump." I watched the smile fade from his face as he slunk down in his chair. Then I felt that familiar tingle on my tongue. . . .

"Mrs. Lutzkraut, maybe *you* should be the witch," I mumbled.

My mouth had done it again. The whole class went silent. I knew she was about to order me to sit recess with her, but what came next was far worse. It felt like a punch in the stomach. She locked eyes with me, gave me a wicked smile, and announced, "Greg will play the role of Robin Hood." Then, to Greg, she asked, "Are you sure you can handle it? After all, you are the play's hero. At the end, you slay the evil Guy of Gisborne and then kiss Jessica. I mean Maid Marian."

What??? I looked over at Greg, who was smiling and definitely seemed like he could handle it. Greg. He had just moved here from California and started at Baber soon after the winter break. He was a perfect Robin Hood, darn it! He was tall, athletic, and the girls all seemed to think he was good-looking. Lately I had gotten the feeling that Jessica liked him better than me. To my added alarm, I could see Jessica blushing and smiling back at him.

"Well, Greg?" Mrs. Lutzkraut asked again.

"No problem, Mrs. L," he replied, his oily voice smooth and confident. "I can handle kissing Maid Marian."

"Excellent, Greg," she said with a sideways look in my direction.

•

I noticed Jessica turn darker red but her smile remained. I wanted to jump out the window.

"Wonderful. Oh, and Greg?"

"Yes?"

"You also will have to kill Rodney."

I shivered. The words *kill* and *Rodney* in the same sentence didn't do wonders for my digestive system.

"Rodney will play Guy of Gisborne." A smile spread across her face as she glanced my way and added, "He'll need to die in the end."

Suddenly my heart began racing, but not because I thought Mrs. Lutzkraut really wanted me dead. She had actually said something far worse. I was going to be playing a character. I would have to speak lines in front of everyone! One of my biggest fears—besides bullies, basements, scary movies, and a hundred other things—is standing up in front of people and talking. Once, in New York, I pretended I was sick for a whole week just to get out of reading my book report to the class.

And just when I thought things couldn't get worse, they did. Mrs. Lutzkraut began to show a PowerPoint presentation of another Robin Hood production she had done a few years ago. As she fiddled with the mouse, a photo of some Merry Men walking on the stage appeared. The costumes were ridiculous. They had hoods and something that looked like short robes, but worst of all, these Merry Men were wearing long yellow tights. I was thinking how bad I felt for that group up there dressed in panty hose when I was struck by an alarming thought.

I was going to be in the same play. Not only did I have to worry about throwing up on the audience when I opened my mouth to speak, but I, too, could wind up wearing tights.

Just as this began to sink in, a sword scene between Robin Hood and the guy I assumed to be Guy of Gisborne twirled onto the screen. It was even worse than I imagined. His tights were powder-blue!

I cringed. I looked over and saw Slim smiling to himself. Evidently he hadn't figured it out yet. Dave, however, sat with a look of horror on his face. He raised his hand.

"Yes, Dave?" Mrs. Lutzkraut asked, clearly annoyed at having her presentation interrupted.

"Uh, Mrs. Lutzkraut, we don't have to wear stockings like them, do we?" he asked.

"They are not wearing stockings. They are wearing authentic tights from the age. That was the look in the medieval time period. We want our play to be visually stunning and genuine. So, yes, you will be wearing them." She went back to clicking and smiling to herself as she looked at the pictures, not noticing the looks we exchanged. The only boy smiling was Toby. A picture on the screen showed a kid pretending to be Friar Tuck. He wore a long brown monk's robe, and if he was wearing tights, they weren't visible. *Our* Friar Tuck looked over at me, winked, and then raised his hand.

"Yes, what is it now?" Mrs. Lutzkraut asked.

Toby turned to her. "My dad has a video camera. I could probably get him to film the whole play."

Mrs. Lutzkraut looked thoughtful. "I think that would be a very good thing to do. I'll speak to you about that later." As she spoke, Toby passed me a note. I read it and gulped. "Is there a problem, Rodney?" Mrs. Lutzkraut snapped.

Toby had only written one little word, but it was enough to make me panic. The note read: "YouTube." It was too much for my brain to handle. I'd be walking around in tights on the Internet for the whole world to see. Half a million people had watched me bravely fly off a cliff on my sled. Now, thanks to Toby, they would all be texting, "Check out Sled Boy's tights." I blurted, "Mrs. Lutzkraut, you can't *really* expect us to wear those outfits!"

"I believe, Rodney, that I already explained about the need for medieval hosen, and since you seem to have difficulty grasping that concept, not to mention every other one, you can join me for lunch today and I'll explain it to you, *again*."

Chapter 14

DODGING MARSHMALLOWS

Later that day, on the bus home, Toby was all smiles. He stood up in the aisle and said, "So, you ballerinas going to dance for us?" He laughed and went to high-five Josh, who sat looking at him with a blank, annoyed expression. "You know, ballerinas," Toby continued. "Dancers?" Josh just sneered. Toby went back to his seat.

His attempted put-down was another reminder of our problem. Kids from all grades were giggling. During lunch, while I dined with Mrs. Lutzkraut, news of Robin Hood and the Merry Wimps spread throughout the school. My friends and I were in trouble. Knocking out Josh, terrorizing the McThuggs, defeating the Ghost of Old Man Johnson, and an epic flight off the Ravine of Doom would all be wiped away the second I walked onstage in my costume.

I was reflecting on this problem when Kayla turned my attention to a different crisis. "Did you hear, Rodney?"

she asked, leaning over me in the aisle. "Greg asked Jessica to go back to his house to practice their lines."

"What?" I couldn't believe it. "They don't even have many lines! She's imprisoned for most of the play."

Kayla smiled, enjoying it. "Yeah, you're right, but they do have *one* very important scene together. You heard Mrs. Lutzkraut. It has to be convincing. Greg thinks it'll be a good idea to practice." I thought my head was going to explode. Kayla's smirk widened, then she spied the boy sitting next to me and her expression changed. "Dave, we should ask Mrs. Lutzkraut if we can be stand-ins for Maid Marian and Robin Hood."

Dave shifted uncomfortably in his seat and asked nervously, "Uh, what's a stand-in?"

"Like, their backups. You know, just in case Jessica and Greg are sick or something. Anyway, we should practice their parts to be ready."

"Uhhh," Dave mumbled.

"Great," Kayla smiled as she headed back over toward Samantha. "I'll come by your house at four thirty."

Dave whispered to me, "Can I come over your house at four twenty?" I heard his words, but my brain was still spinning from the thoughts of Greg's practice sessions.

By the next day things had gotten even worse. At recess—which I was allowed to attend—we came together and discussed the problem. No one wanted to do the performance. My mention of Toby's note put them into a real panic.

"We have to do something," Slim piped up. This was met by unanimous agreement.

"But what?" Dave asked, which brought on a nervous silence. Gradually their eyes shifted in my direction. Dave continued, "Well, Rodney, what should we do?"

"How should *I* know?" I asked.

"You'll think of something," Slim added. "You always do."

"Me? I'm not the brains of the group. Rishi's the one always thinks up what to do next."

"True, I am a bit of an idea guy," Rishi agreed. "That's why I'm not at all worried about this situation." Dave smiled for the first time in two days, and Slim let out a sigh. "I'm not worried because I know Rodney will figure something out." Dave and Slim nodded in agreement. Sometimes I wanted to bang their heads together.

"Why are you guys worrying yourselves?" I looked up and saw Greg holding his lunch tray. "We're really lucky to be putting on the play," he explained. "It beats long division and editing essays."

Slim snapped, "Didn't you see the slides, Mr. Hood? You're going to be in tights, too."

"So what? I've got nice legs. Besides, the girls are excited to see us wearing them. *Jessica* told me this morning that she couldn't wait to see me in the dress rehearsal. Anyway, I'll see you guys later. Oh yeah," he exclaimed, looking at the other end of the table. "Thanks, Toby, for offering to give me a copy of the video."

"No problem, Greg," Toby answered, looking at me with a slight smile. I wanted to pelt the two of them with today's chicken nuggets.

By the time I got to gym class, I was so jealous that I actually confronted Jessica. We were playing what my old school had called Dodgeball, but at Baber it was named "Happy Marshmallow Ball" because the government here had outlawed Dodgeball. It never made sense to me, especially since both games used the same red playground balls. I walked over to Jessica and whispered, "What are you doing with Greg?"

Jessica dodged a Happy Marshmallow. "What do you mean? And why are you so red?"

"You know, your big practice sessions. What are you doing at his house?"

"Well, he actually came over to *my* house, and he only came over once."

That made me feel a little better, but not much. One question still burned in my brain. I wanted to play it cool but couldn't. "What exactly did you practice?"

Jessica smiled and asked, "Why should it matter to you?"

She had me there. I tried to decide if I should tell her that I liked her. I began to open my mouth but she spoke first.

"He wanted to practice the kiss scene but my dad saw him and sent him home."

Greatly relieved, I told her the truth. "Your dad sounds like a great guy."

Jessica laughed. "He is. It looks like I'll only be kissing Greg during the dress rehearsal."

Just as my brain wrestled with that one, a Happy Marshmallow smashed me right in the face.

Chapter 15

SWEET REVENGE

The day of the play was Friday, February 14. Not only was it Valentine's Day, it was the day before Presidents' Week. Normally it's a pretty darn good time because we get off from school to celebrate Washington and Lincoln. There was nothing good about it this year. With all my various problems weighing on me, I grew more and more depressed as the day got closer. Not only was I worried about wearing tights and afraid I would lose Jessica to Greg, but I had found out that Rocco and his family were arriving any day.

On Thursday, February 13, we had a dress rehearsal. It was awful. The tights looked more ridiculous in person than they had in the pictures. Friar Tuck thought it was hysterical, and throughout the action we heard him snickering to himself. We were without hope, and though Mrs. Lutzkraut criticized our acting, she thought the tights looked great.

Toby wasn't alone in his enjoyment. Greg strutted around in his green outfit, and Kayla—dressed like an evil witch—chased Will Scarlet between scenes trying to pinch his legs. I felt like running offstage. The one bright spot was that Greg had to leave early to go to the dentist, sparing me from witnessing two days of him kissing Jessica.

Upon arriving home that day I was met by the whirlwind otherwise known as my great-aunt Evelyn. I didn't know she was coming. In fact, none of us did. That's what she did. She'd whisk into town on a whim and everything instantly revolved around her. She was a lot of fun, but in my funk, she really had to work to get me going.

"There's my darling nephew!" she exclaimed as I opened the front door.

"Aunt Evelyn, what are you doing here?" I asked.

"I hear you are now a big actor, and I came to see the performance tomorrow." I looked over at my mom, who smiled at her aunt and me. I frowned.

"I really don't want to be in the play. We have to wear these awful tights and everyone will make fun of us," I complained. My aunt smiled and turned to me.

"Errol Flynn wore tights, you know. Ah, Rodney, you'll be great, and I have something for you." She swooped into the dining room and I stumbled behind, wondering who Errol Flynn was. She pulled out a big red, heart-shaped box.

"You got me chocolates?" I asked.

"Rodney, this box of chocolates comes all the way from Brussels where I was visiting the prince. Brussels is the capital of Belgium, by the way, and Rodney, you may not know this, but they make some of the best chocolate in the world there. This box in particular has the finest, richest chocolate money can buy. It will make any girl faint from happiness when it touches her lips. So I brought it for you to give. Your mom let me know there's a little girl that you fancy." I reddened and glanced back at my mom, who looked away.

"I can't bring that to school. The other . . ."

"Hush," my great-aunt said, gently putting her finger on my lips. "Rodney, you can bring it. Trust your auntie, she knows what's good for you."

"Thanks, Aunt Evelyn, but I think she might like another boy."

"All the more reason to give it to her, then. One bite and she'll melt. Now, enough talk. Let's mambo!"

"Huh?" I asked.

"Rodney, it's time I teach you one of the world's best dances," she said, grabbing me by the shoulders, pressing PLAY on the stereo, and dragging me to the center of the living room. "Now we mambo!" And we did. And it was fun. And for a little while I forgot about Rocco, Jessica, tights, Greg, and YouTube.

Aunt Evelyn did a good job of keeping my mind from the approaching fiasco, but morning eventually came, and with it, dread. I set out for school with a heavy heart and backpack full of chocolates. In the back of Mrs. Lutzkraut's class, while taking out our books, Aunt Evelyn's box of chocolates caught Slim's eye.

"What's that, Rodney?" he asked, pointing at the box. It was large and took up most of the room in my pack. I was still debating if I was really going to give it to Jessica, but now it was noticed, and Toby was always around to jump on a situation.

"Ooooh, who's your valentine, Rodney?" he said, grabbing it and holding it to his chest. "Is it Rishi?"

I snatched it back and felt my cheeks reddening. I met Jessica's eyes. She looked down at the box. Other students had gathered and were looking at me holding the box. My mouth felt dry and my knees started to shake slightly. I had to make a decision. I decided to . . .

"What's all this commotion?" Mrs. Lutzkraut snapped, eyeing the box in my hands. I thought I saw her lick her lips for a second as she held out her hand. "This is causing quite a disruption. I'll hold on to it for safekeeping." I didn't know what to say as she snatched Aunt Evelyn's chocolates from me. I was confused, embarrassed, and mad. An already bad day had just gotten worse . . . and the play wasn't even scheduled until 2:00 p.m.

At lunch, everyone started panicking, beginning with Dave. "What are we going to do?" he screamed. "I can't handle another day of wearing tights around Kayla."

"We've got to do something," Rishi shouted. "Rodney, you must have an idea!"

Toby interrupted us with, "He's got nothing. You boys are going to be the joke of the school. It's going to be . . ." He continued on and on, but I stopped listening. Instead I was thinking that we had to make one last appeal to Mrs. Lutzkraut. If I explained our position, maybe, just maybe, she might listen. I doubted I would succeed, but I also figured that if I annoyed her enough she might kick me out of the performance.

I stood up. Everyone at the lunch table stopped what they were doing and looked in my direction. "I think I know how to save us." They were all silent as I headed out of the cafeteria. The aides, as usual, were too busy talking to even notice me.

I trudged up the stairs and down the silent, empty hall to my class. I peered in. Mrs. Lutzkraut was there at her desk all right, but the sight shocked me. She was holding her stomach and moaning. Empty chocolate wrappers littered her desk and covered the floor. It seemed as if she had brown lipstick smeared crazily all around her mouth. Her eyes fluttered, and with a shudder and a gurgle her head fell forward and came to rest on top of a big red, very familiar-looking heart-shaped chocolate box.

I was about to approach her to make sure she was all right, but then she rubbed her stomach and moaned. I ran to get Mr. Feebletop. I found him in his office busy counting baseball cards. After explaining what I had just witnessed, he thanked me for getting him. Before heading off with the nurse, he turned back and looked like he was struggling to find the right words. "This could be very embarrassing for Mrs. Lutzkraut—" he began.

Before he could go on, I said, "Don't worry. I won't tell anyone."

He was greatly relieved. "Thanks, Rodney," he said with a smile. "I owe you one."

"Well, Mr. Feebletop, if that's how you feel, there *is* something you can do."

"Oh. What's that, Rodney?"

"Well you see, Mr. Feebletop . . ."

When I got back to recess, the aides were still too busy talking to notice me, and I soon found my friends. They immediately gathered around me and demanded to know what had happened. Before I could tell them, Long Nose blew the whistle and we lined up. We stood there silently, forbidden to talk, and we—well, not really me—were surprised after a while to see Mr. Feebletop come to pick us up.

We trailed him in the hall and some of the boys looked at me curiously. No one knew what was going on as we entered our classroom and sat down. Mr. Feebletop waited for everyone to settle, glanced at the custodian who was busy sweeping something up, and cleared his throat.

"Mrs. Lutzkraut had to leave school for the day. It's

rather sad, being that today is the day of the big performance, but she should be all right."

"What happened, Mr. Feebletop?" Jessica asked.

"Well, young lady, let's just say she had to leave for the day." Now all the boys were looking at me. A couple of them actually looked scared. Rishi's eyes were bugging out of his head, and Toby looked at me dumbstruck, his ugly mouth hanging open even wider than usual. Mr. Feebletop continued, "We cannot postpone the play, since all your parents have already begun to arrive. I'll be helping out in Mrs. Lutzkraut's absence. The show must go on, without her."

I coughed.

"Oh yes. One more thing. I've been thinking about the final scene with Maid Marian and Robin Hood. I think kissing at a school performance is inappropriate. I think it would be better, if after rescuing Maid Marian, Robin Hood gives her a nice handshake."

"But Mr. Feebletop," Greg blurted.

"I've made my decision, young man. A handshake, and that's it."

I coughed again.

"Oh, and it seems the play is running a bit long, so I have decided to eliminate the speech by Clark Griswold at the end."

"Uh, that's Guy of Gisborne," I corrected him.

"Yes, okay. Anyway, I hope that's fine with you, Rodney."

I flashed a brief look of disappointment but told him I understood. When it looked as though he was finished talking I caught his eye and coughed one last time, even louder than before.

"Oh yes. It has come to my attention that there is a problem with some of the team uniforms. . . ."

"Costumes."

"Thank you, Rodney. Yes, costumes. It seems the tights that you are supposed to wear are a bit too small. I hope you don't mind, but I'm suggesting that you wear your jeans instead."

The boys in the class broke into a cheer and jumped up—except, of course, for Toby. Mr. Feebletop then led us down to the stage, where the other boys gathered around me.

"I knew you'd do it," Rishi spoke for them all. "But *how* did you do it?"

"You know, Rishi," I answered, "let's just say I have my ways," and I didn't elaborate. This time none of them created stories to explain what had happened. Whatever I had done was beyond their imaginations.

The performance turned out to be a hit, and most of my male classmates were forever grateful to me. One who wasn't happy was a very grumpy Friar Tuck, who did a lousy job of living up to the title of Merry Man.

I was ecstatic. Especially as I watched a gloomy Robin Hood give Maid Marian a dejected handshake.

Afterward, Jessica came over to me. "Well, it's over. Funny how things turned out."

"What do you mean?" I asked.

"A handshake? You're really something, Rodney Rathbone." She laughed and reached out and gave me a handshake.

"Save me, Rodney!" Dave ran by with his witch hot in pursuit, looking for a Valentine's Day handshake of her own.

Later that night, Aunt Evelyn insisted on taking our family out for a big dinner to celebrate. She kept saying that the performance rivaled anything she had seen in all the great theaters of Europe. At one point, while waiting for our appetizers, she leaned over to me and asked, "So, were the chocolates a hit?"

I smiled and answered, "Yes, Aunt Evelyn, they certainly were. I guess you could say they stole the show."

She smiled back and I felt great. It had been some day. I was even acting nice to Penny. We were all having a good time, except my mother, who looked like she had something bad to say. As soon as our waitress cleared the dinner plates, I wasn't surprised to hear my mom announce, "I'm afraid I have some disappointing news."

"There's no dessert?" my father asked, looking alarmed.

My mother continued. "Rodney, this concerns you."

"What's the matter?"

"I got a call today from Mrs. Ronboni."

My stomach tightened. "Yeah?"

"The Ronbonis won't be coming out this week. It seems they've all come down with the hyena flu. It's worse than either the swine flu or bird flu. Poor Rocco is real sick."

"How awful," I said, putting on a fake sad voice. I did my best to fight off the smile that threatened to crack the sides of my lips.

My mom nodded her head slightly and said, "I can see this has really upset you, Rodney. Don't worry, though. Mrs. Ronboni said they'd reschedule the trip. And do you know what else?"

I shook my head, fearing what she'd say next.

"Rocco wanted his mom to give you a special message. He said he can't wait to come for you. That he's looking forward to making up for lost time. He said you'd understand."

I understood all right. I squirmed in my seat, dreading those wedgies that were heading my way.

Chapter 16

THE BATHROOM

Following Presidents' break, Mrs. Lutzkraut never mentioned the chocolates or the fact that we wore jeans under our robes. All she said was that the faculty had complimented the show, and then she dropped the subject. I figured she was embarrassed about her feeding frenzy and wanted to move on.

And we did. In no time at all we were right back to our normal, boring classroom routine. It gave me plenty of time to worry about the Ronbonis' trip, but at least everything in Ohio was pretty much business as usual for the next few weeks—until I began to notice little things that bothered me.

For instance, there was one day in early March when it was warm enough for us to go outside for recess. I was playing basketball and chased down a loose ball. Out of the corner of my eye I saw Josh shoving some kid around on the field. I pretended not to notice. Later that week everyone was talking about Josh cornering a kid in the hallway and demanding his lunch money. Suddenly my chicken sense kicked in. Things were changing. Josh was back to his bullying self. Not when I was around, but he was starting to feel comfortable, and that could only spell trouble for me.

Trouble came knocking two days later. I was home lying on the couch. That morning I had woken up with a stomachache—after worrying about Josh and Rocco all night—and convinced my mom to let me stay home. Besides, a day on the couch was a lot better than even a few minutes with Mrs. Lutzkraut. That is, until there was a knock on the door at around four thirty. My mom answered it.

"Hi, Mrs. Rathbone. Can we see Rodney?" It was Rishi's voice.

"Rishi, Rodney's been sick, maybe tomor—"

"Mrs. Rathbone, thanks for letting us in. It's really important." My mom just sighed and walked away as my three friends barged into the living room. "You feeling better, Rodney?"

"A little." The truth is that my stomachache had disappeared as soon as my mom had said I could stay home.

"That's good, 'cause we need you back at school," Rishi went on.

"Why, does Mrs. Lutzkraut miss me?" I joked.

"No, Josh is acting up really bad," Rishi answered seriously.

Just then my father came in from work. "Who's acting up?" he asked, taking off his coat.

"This bully, Josh. Today he even took our back seats on the bus."

"Yeah, and he called me Flabio," Slim whined.

My father asked, "Rodney, isn't Josh the kid you knocked out on the first day of school?"

"That's the one," Rishi answered for me. My stomachache was returning.

"So, you coming back tomorrow?" Rishi continued.

"Well, this stomach of mine is . . ."

"Better," my dad interrupted. "He'll be on the bus tomorrow. If there's one thing my son isn't, it's a coward."

"You got that right, Mr. Rathbone," Dave agreed. "I don't know where we'd be without him."

I just groaned and rolled over.

The next day my friends made me join them in the back of the bus. When Josh climbed aboard, Rishi was waiting for him. "Where you sitting today?"

Josh glared back at him, but he noticed me sitting there, and while I tried hard not to pull the emergency latch and jump out the back door, he eventually sat down in the middle.

"That's what I thought!" Rishi yelled.

Great. Josh was already getting itchy. The last thing I needed was Rishi egging him on. My brain was entering crisis mode and it wasn't long before the rest of my body followed.

By the time I got into class, my stomach was rumbling pretty bad. Cramps tightened my lower stomach. I could feel gurgling and pressure building. It was all I could do to keep from farting. I sat there sweating and clenching and praying nothing sneaked out. To fart in class would lead to weeks, no months, maybe even years of jokes. The one math equation I did understand was that

a fart = funny

but not for the person who lets one slip.

With each passing thought of Josh beating my face to a pulp, the chance of me passing gas increased.

Mrs. Lutzkraut didn't let us use the restroom. She told us that there was time before school, during lunch, and after school. Emergencies, according to her, were the result of bad planning, and therefore didn't really exist in her mind. Art was coming up, so I bit down on my pencil eraser and held on.

The walk to art was difficult. Rishi whispered, "What's the matter with your legs?" I must have been walking funny.

"Nothing," I muttered through clenched teeth.

We filed into art class and while everyone else went to sit down, I went straight up to Mr. Borus. "Can I go to the bathroom?"

"*May I*," he replied.

"May I go to the bathroom?" I said correctly.

"Yes, you may," he answered. I zoomed out of the room and did some sort of speed duckwalk to the bathroom. I passed the sinks and urinals, went to the last of the three stalls, locked the door, and was about to unbutton my pants when I heard the boys' room door smash open. Two voices made me temporarily forget my bathroom woes. Toby was speaking and Josh was grunting.

I felt uneasy, to say the least. Despite his leaving me alone, Josh was still big and seemed to hate me with his whole heart. Hearing Toby spitting out my name made a scary situation considerably worse.

"I'm telling you, Josh, Rodney's nothing." I caught my breath. I probably could have walked out past them, given them a mean look, and been out of there, but I froze and stood quiet.

"You keep saying that, but I don't seeing *you* doing anything," Josh bitterly reminded Toby.

"I've tried everything! I got him to go into the McThuggs' yard, I got . . ."

Josh interrupted him. "Yeah, Tobe, I was there for most of it. How did all those things turn out? I seem to remember the McThuggs running away from him. He hung out in Old Man Johnson's for like an hour and who knows what he did to Mrs. Lutzkraut that day of the play! You said you had him with those dumb tights. . . ."

Toby responded, "I did. It was all set. Yellow tights, my dad recording it, how was I . . ."

"If he's nothing, then how's he doing all this stuff?" Josh finally asked. I was curious too. All my attention was on their words and I had forgotten about my other issues.

Toby said, "I mean, he's not tough. He's smart. He seems to be able . . ."

"Not tough! Are you saying I'm not tough?" I heard some shuffling and what sounded like a choking sound.

"Nouunnnnnhh no yaaaarr," Toby tried to speak, but something, or someone, was making it difficult. Finally after some coughs and sniffs he wheezed, "Man, you didn't have to do that. You're the toughest here. That's my point! Gosh!"

Josh grunted and said, "For not being tough, he managed to break my nose and knock me out, remember?" As he said "remember" it sounded like he shoved Toby into the wall. "I had a headache for a month," he continued. "I'm not getting hit like that again. Maybe you should try to fight him if you're so confident." There was a long silence. "That's what I thought."

In listening to their conversation I had forgotten that another part of me had something big to say, and when it came out it would be no silent squeaker. It would be a big blast. I knew I was caught but jumped up onto the toilet to hide my legs.

"Who's in here?" Josh screamed. I didn't say anything, convinced that I was finally done for. When they caught me in the stall hiding, they'd know Toby had been right, that I wasn't a tough guy. What tough guy hid in a bathroom stall?

"Who's in here?" Josh demanded a second time. "Toby, look under there!" Fear had me like a vise. Almost in a trance I stopped breathing and looked at the graffiti and boogers on the back of the door and held my breath.

"There's no legs," Toby told Josh.

"Kick the doors open!" Josh yelled. Toby must have paused, for Josh continued, "Out of my way. I'll do it!" Just then I heard the first of the three stalls slam open hard. The whole frame seemed to shake and some plaster fell from the ceiling onto my hair.

"I'll do the next one!" Toby sniped. They were at the second stall. Soon they'd be up to mine, and I'd be done for. I heard the kick but it seemed as if the door hadn't opened at all.

"Nice kick, girly."

"Well," Toby whined defensively, "I think it's locked."

"Oh, is it? Then I'll kick that lock right off." A deafening explosion shook the bathroom. The door of the stall next to mine practically flew off its hinges. "Looky, looky. Well it seems this little kid's been listening to us. You been listenin'?"

"Ahh," a little scared voice squeaked.

"That's what I thought. What should we do with this little spy, Toby?"

"The toilet's right there," Toby suggested.

"You know, Tobe, I knew there was a reason I liked you," Josh answered.

At this point the kid, whoever he was, started crying and made a break for it. I heard him trip and fall flat to the floor but he was up in an instant and out the door. Josh and Toby were cracking up.

"Hey look!" Toby laughed. "Diarrhea of a wimpy kid." That got them laughing even harder.

"Just like old times," Toby said as the laughs dwindled.

"Good times," Josh answered.

"Times that could come again, if only someone was taken care of," Toby said, getting more serious.

"You're back to that now, Toby?"

"Josh, if I can prove that Rodney isn't all that tough, will you pound him? Just think about how good we had it before."

There was a long pause, but finally Josh replied, "Toby, if you can somehow prove that, well, there's no one I'd rather hurt than Rodney Rathbone. It'd be a dream come true." They were both quiet for a minute. Then Josh added, "I'd better get back to class."

"Oh man, Mr. Borus is waitin' for me, too. Let's go." After a minute the door slammed shut, leaving me in silence. It wasn't silent for long, however. With an explosion that almost shook the tiles off the walls, I finally did what I had come in there for.

Chapter 17

THE MOVIES, GIRLS, and CANNIBALISTIC DEATH MUTANTS

So, I was dead meat. I would have to be careful around Josh and Toby. I'd need to be tough in every way. I couldn't walk into a trap or let anything distract me. I'd focus completely on the situation. Nothing would break my concentration . . . not blond hair blowing in the breeze, not blue eyes looking over at me, not even a sly smile in my direction. . . .

Where was I going with this? Oh yeah, I couldn't let anything distract me. But it was such a pleasant distraction, and no matter how hard I tried, my thoughts kept returning to Jessica—and this problem I was having. You see, while I should have been walking around flexing my muscles, giving Toby menacing looks, and e-mailing bad articles about Ohio to Rocco's mother, I spent half the time trying to get closer to Jessica. Only whenever I did, Mrs. Lutzkraut or Greg or Kayla or even Rishi would somehow foil my moves. Then one day I got my chance. It came in late March during recess when I happened to overhear the girls talking.

"Let's go to the movies on Saturday," Kayla was telling Samantha and Jessica.

"I'm in," Jessica answered. "What time?"

I moved a little closer, wanting to hear more.

"We should go early, maybe right after dinner," Kayla suggested. "Let's find out when *Animal Boy* is playing. I hear it's so funny. Ask your parents and let me know tomorrow. I'm sure my dad can drive us."

This was getting interesting. Running into Jessica "by accident" at the movies would give me a chance to see her without Mrs. Lutzkraut or that jerky Greg lurking over my shoulder. Everyone, including my three best friends, had really started to like Greg, but not me. He was my competition, and I was suspicious of his surfer charm and permanent tan.

Back in class, I fought off thoughts of movie theaters and girls and tried to listen to Mrs. Lutzkraut's boring math lesson, but after a few minutes I looked over at Jessica. My mind immediately went to Saturday. If only I could see her at the movies, I could talk to her for a while and maybe even sit next to her in the dark theater. . . .

"Rodney!" snapped a familiar, nasty voice.

"Yes, Mrs. Lutzkraut?"

"What do you call the bottom number of a fraction?"

"Jessica," I blurted out. I meant to say *denominator*, of course, but it was too late. The whole class started laughing and I could feel my cheeks get red hot. Rishi was whooping, the girls were giggling, and Greg was rolling his eyes. Jessica, by the way, was also a bit red and looked down into her textbook.

"That's enough!" Mrs. Lutzkraut snapped and the room silenced even faster than it had erupted. "Rodney, are you allergic to paying attention? Maybe you'll be able to learn the parts of a fraction if there are no young ladies around to distract you. Plan on joining me for recess tomorrow!" I almost said, "Great, I'll bring the chocolates," but thought better of it and kept my mouth shut for the rest of the day.

On the bus ride home my friends teased me about my answer in math. Rishi kept asking, "What is the least common Jessica of one-half and two-thirds," which even made *me* laugh. After a while, though, I was ready to change the subject and decided to bring up the movies. My friends thought going on Saturday was a great idea, and Slim and Dave agreed that *Animal Boy* was a good choice. Rishi, however, wanted to see *Cannibalistic Mutants of Death Eat New York*.

"That movie looks so dumb," I said, wanting to be near Jessica on Saturday and, just as important, cannibals and mutants didn't sound like my idea of a good time.

"Are you kidding? It looks awesome," Rishi replied.

Slim added, "Yeah, you get to see them eat brains!" That not only spooked me, it turned my stomach.

"I think it's rated *R*, though," Dave pointed out. "We can't get into that show."

Way to go, Dave, I thought. Eventually Rishi agreed that *Animal Boy* wasn't a bad second option. All we needed to do now was check with our parents and get someone to drive.

Later that night at the dinner table I brought up the movies. My parents didn't mind, so I asked if they could take us. My dad, who was making a puddle of gravy in his mashed potatoes, acted like he didn't hear me. My mom, however, made a face.

"I don't know, Rodney. I made plans to have the Windbaggers over for dinner that night. . . ."

"I'll take you boys!" my dad volunteered, practically spitting out his pork chop. His hearing had suddenly improved.

"Donald, you *know* Fred and Ethel are coming over, and Fred wants to talk to you about insurance, remember?"

My dad looked like he was trying to swallow something rotten and replied, "This is our son we're talking about here. I'm most concerned with his well-being, and if I have to sacrifice a couple of things that I've been looking forward to . . . well . . . that's what being a parent is all about. Isn't it?"

My mom sighed. I doubted she was buying any of my dad's nonsense, and I really didn't care. All I knew was that my plan had been set in motion.

As I walked away from the dinner table, Penny followed me into the den. "What do you want?" I asked. "You're not coming to the movies with us!"

"No kidding. I was going to tell you something important, but never mind now."

"What could you possibly tell me?" I teased her. "That you're mean and short and . . ."

"Greg is planning to ask out Jessica."

"What?" I yelled. I felt the blood drain from my face, but not wanting her to know how I really felt, I asked more calmly, "Really? That sounds nice. I doubt she's interested in him, though. Anyway, how do *you* know so much?"

"I'm friends with his sister, Sunshine."

"Sunshine? What kind of name is that?"

Penny frowned. "It's a nice name, and Greg's like the best-looking kid in town, so I know she's interested. I thought I'd tell you so you can give up on her. Not that you had a shot anyway . . ."

"I got a shot! Uhh, I mean I'm not interested so it doesn't really make any difference."

"Then how come you say her name when you're sleeping?"

"What? I don't do that!" *Do I?* I thought.

She was smiling at me now, clearly enjoying the moment. "Have nice dreams tonight, Rodney." She walked off to her room.

I hated to admit it to myself, but I believed what

she said. I wondered whether I really did have a shot at Jessica. The more I thought about it, the more I realized that my movie plan had better work. I kept going over it in my head. Before drifting off to sleep, I turned face-down into the pillow. It was hard to breathe, and I was pretty sure I'd suffocate, but at least Penny wouldn't hear me calling anyone's name out.

Chapter 18

FRIGHT NIGHT

For almost an hour on Saturday my dad kept yelling up the stairs, "Aren't you ready to leave for the movies yet?"

"Relax!" I shouted back. "I told the guys we would pick them up at five and it's only four thirty."

"Well, it's always better to arrive early than late," he muttered nervously.

"I wonder if the Windbaggers feel that way about their dinner invitation," I teased him.

My mom had invited them to come a bit later so my dad could see them. Now he was in a complete panic. "Let's get a move on, Rodney!"

The truth of the matter is that I was busy looking for just the right shirt to impress Jessica and had even spent a little extra time on the hair. To my father's great relief we finally headed out to pick up my friends. I noticed Rishi eye my slick hair as he got into the car, but luckily he kept his mouth shut. I was nervous enough about how I'd act with Jessica without him teasing me. Heavy raindrops began pelting the windshield as we drove off to the big multiplex theater at the mall.

Most of the way there, Dave and Slim were quiet while Rishi kept up a steady conversation with my father. I, on the other hand, split my thoughts between hoping we would run into the girls and praying we didn't run into any undesirable types, like Greg the Magnificent. Suddenly I focused on what Rishi was saying to my dad.

"The movie you're seeing, Mr. Rathbone. What's it called again?"

"What?" I shouted. "Dad, you can't go to the movies with us!"

"Relax, son. What I said is that I'm seeing a documentary on fast food. Apparently, they're finding that some of that stuff is bad for you."

Even if it was a different movie, I wasn't exactly thrilled about my dad being under the same multiplex roof. Not tonight, at least. "Aren't the Windbaggers coming over?" I reminded him.

"Well, I thought you might need an adult around tonight."

"Dad, we don't need . . . ," I began.

"Now, now. I don't plan on holding your hand, but it's important for parents to spend time with their children, and tonight is a bit dark and stormy. Look at that thunder and lightning. What kind of a father would I be if I just dropped you off?"

I knew my dad too well to buy this whole noble act. "Trying to avoid an insurance conversation?" I asked him.

"Like the plague," he replied.

By the time we got to the mall, it was pouring and the sky was as dark as night. We made a dash for it through the parking lot and a lightning bolt hit so close that some car alarms went off. I hoped the storm wouldn't keep the girls away.

After buying the tickets, we hung out in the lobby for a minute until my father walked off. I saw Rishi look down the corridor that had entrances to the different theaters. I, too, was looking for something, and there by the orange neon lights of the concession counter I saw her.

"Guys, do you want to get popcorn?" I asked.

"What do you think, Rodney?" Slim asked while pushing me aside. "Extra butter, here I come!"

As we approached where the girls were standing, Samantha noticed me and called out, "Hey look, it's our star math student in person." Everyone laughed.

"Is Greg with you guys?" Jessica asked. That one pierced my heart like a dagger.

"No, he isn't," I said flatly.

Kayla walked over. "Hi, Dave. Why don't you sit with us?"

"Sounds like a great idea," I blurted, a little too enthusiastically.

Rishi put his arm around my shoulder and whispered, "I see what you're up to, but you'd better leave the rest to me. I'm the professional here and I have an idea that will get Jessica right where you want her."

Before I could ask what he was up to—I never trusted Rishi's bright ideas—the multiplex suddenly went dark and thunder boomed through the walls. All the girls screamed and my heart started racing. With a flicker, the lights came back on. "That was weird," I said to Rishi, secretly relieved. "Anyway, what's this idea you were about to mention?"

The popcorn guy interrupted us with, "What you want?"

"Everything," Slim answered. By the time he finished blowing a year's worth of allowance on junk, it was my turn. I ordered an ultra-mega popcorn and something called a Super-Vente Deluxe Coke, which cost like twenty bucks and was the size of a fish tank. I turned back to Rishi but he was already heading off.

We rejoined the girls, handed our tickets to a yawning teenager, and began walking down the long blue hallway where we could see the sign for *Animal Boy* lit up at the end. I was thinking about how I was going to sit next to Jessica when Rishi set his plan in motion.

"Look, guys, there's no one around," he began.

"So?" Kayla asked.

"Don't you see? We can sneak into *Cannibalistic Mutants of Death Eat New York*. It's starting in two minutes."

"It's rated *R*," I reminded him. The last thing I needed was some scary movie.

"Actually, it's not *R*," Kayla pointed out. "It's *PG*-13. Look at the sign."

"Excellent!" Rishi shouted. "Let's go in. The two movies are on at the same time. The *Mutants* will rock—"

"Yeah," I interrupted, "but I'm not sure the girls really want to see *Cann*—"

"I'll check out the *Mutants*," Jessica announced, and that ended that.

As we walked in, Rishi whispered to me, "Isn't this great? You're going to owe me big-time."

"What's so great about it?" I whispered back.

"Come on, Rodney, everyone knows if you sit next to a girl in a horror movie, she's going to be scared." He then hit me in the chest. "You'll have to, you know, protect her. See? I'm always watching out for you. Great plan, right?"

"Dave! You have to sit next to me," Kayla interrupted.

"Uh," Dave responded nervously.

"You don't want the mutants to get me, do you?"

"Well . . ." I could see the wheels in his head starting to turn.

"Good." Kayla smiled, and with that she dragged him inside the theater doors.

"See? She understands my brilliance," Rishi continued. "Now it's your turn, but you'd better hurry or Slim will be munching and burping next to Jessica for the next two hours."

The girls and Kayla's prisoner had entered a row toward the front. I was relieved to see that Jessica went in last, but alarmed to see Slim beginning to follow her. I ran down the slope as fast as I could, the little lights on the floor whizzing by beneath my feet. At the row's entrance I hip-checked Slim. He looked annoyed for a second, then went, "Oh, I get it."

The plan was working to perfection, though I half-expected Mrs. Lutzkraut to be in the row behind us.

I couldn't believe I was finally next to Jessica in the dark. It was so awesome that my mind went completely blank. I didn't know what to say. The two of us sat staring in silence at an ad on the screen for Larry's Transmissions. This was ridiculous. Luckily, Rishi elbowed me and pointed to the large popcorn I was holding. I think he wanted it, but my mind sprang into action and I offered the popcorn to Jessica. She took some and offered me her Sno-Caps. During the exchange our hands briefly touched. It was a magical moment that sent tingles down my neck, until I started worrying that my fingers were too greasy from the butter.

Soon the coming attractions were on and then the movie started. Most of my attention was on the girl to my left and I wondered if she was thinking similar thoughts about the boy on her right.

On the screen, a scientist was shouting, "If we don't destroy this serum it will destroy the world!"

He was answered by another character wearing a

suit who looked more like a businessman than a scientist. "The company I represent has spent far too much money to let you do that. Hand me the serum."

"Never! You don't understand what . . ." They went on like that, but in the end the businessman wrestled the serum away from the scientist, only to walk outside, slip on a patch of ice, and release the serum's vapors into the air. Of course, the guys who breathed in the vapor turned into cannibalistic mutants of death and ran off looking for people to eat.

Now, in the past, there's no way you would have found me watching a movie like this, but I suddenly felt like I would enter a real-live den of cannibalistic mutants if it meant saving Jessica. Or, at least I'd wish her well before running off. But the point is, I had accomplished a lot this year and maybe I wasn't such a huge coward after all.

As the film went on, I sat there trying to figure out whether I should reach for Jessica's hand. My thoughts, however, were interrupted by something on the screen. A lady was walking down a dark basement hallway and you could tell she was about to get it. It was one frightening place. Water dripped and creepy, screechy music played. There was thunder in the distance and I couldn't tell if the thunder was in the movie or real life. I could barely breathe I was so petrified. For a moment there was complete silence. Then it happened.

A mutant suddenly jumped out and squeezed my arm!

I screamed and jumped up, flinging the popcorn bucket onto Jessica's head and my Coke into her lap. She screamed, and the next thing I knew we were all screaming and tearing out of the theater.

It was only as we rushed into the hallway that it occurred to me what had happened. Rishi knew his stuff all right, for the movie had frightened Jessica so much that she had grabbed my arm. That would have been great and exactly what I wanted, if only . . . if only I wasn't convinced I was being clawed to death by a cannibalistic mutant.

I looked around the hallway. Rishi was shaking Slim, who was pale and on the verge of fainting. Kayla was grabbing Dave, even though she didn't look as scared as the rest of us. It took at least a minute for everyone else to stop screaming, and then our attention turned to Jessica. She had removed the popcorn bucket from her head but was covered in kernels and her face was shiny from all the grease. She also looked like she had wet her pants, but I knew it was Coke. My Coke.

She walked up to me and said, "Real smooth move."

"I'm sorry, I didn't mean to do it. The mutant scared me," I tried to explain.

She looked angry. "*You* were afraid? I thought the great Rodney Rathbone wasn't afraid of anything. Come on, girls, lets get out of here." As they walked off, I realized that my plan had completely backfired.

For a while we hung around making dumb small talk

waiting for my dad's film to end. As soon as he saw us he came over and asked, "Who's hungry?"

"I am!" Slim yelled. Evidently he had made a quick recovery.

"How about we go get some salads," my dad suggested.

"Salads?" Slim blurted.

"I've sworn off fast food after seeing that movie."

"Even White Castle?" Slim asked.

"Mmmmmmm . . . White Castle," my dad murmured, sounding a lot like Homer Simpson. "Okay, White Castle can't be that bad, right? Let's go."

But I had lost my appetite. Noticing my lousy mood, Rishi said to me, "Don't worry about it. She didn't seem that mad."

I looked at him. He looked away and said, "Well, maybe she *was* that mad. Too bad you ordered the mega soda and popcorn."

Too bad was right. I had nightmares that evening of cute mutant girls throwing Cokes at me. I awoke to a depressed feeling as the knowledge sunk in that I'd really blown it. Not only with Jessica, but with everyone. Kayla had probably called Greg the second she got home. News of my stunt would be the talk of school on Monday. Toby would make the most of it and convince Josh that I was an easy target. I almost didn't want to go downstairs when my mom called me for Sunday breakfast.

"So," she greeted me, pouring a glass of orange juice, "your father tells me you had a great time at the movies last night."

My dad had avoided the Windbaggers, watched a documentary, and inhaled half a dozen burgers at White Castle. To him, that was like going to the moon. But as for me, well, all I could say was, "Sure, Mom. It was some night."

Chapter 19

AS BAD AS IT GETS

My legs were slow to sling out of bed Monday morning. When they finally did, I stared down at my feet and the blue carpet squeezing up between my toes. For several seconds I pondered the fibers . . . and the upcoming day.

I'd soon know whether Jessica was completely turned off by my girly scream on Saturday night. All my questions would be answered as soon as I got to school, like how far the news had actually spread. If the story was out there, would slimy Greg use it to move in on Jessica? Would the kids realize I wasn't so brave after all? Would Josh use this opportunity to pound my face into hamburger meat?

Almost like a zombie, I climbed aboard the bus and shuffled back to my friends. "What's the matter with you?" Rishi asked. "You look so serious."

"Well," I exhaled, "Saturday didn't exactly go as planned. You know I . . ."

"I know if there's one person who doesn't need to worry about something like this, it's you. Who's going to care about a little scream? We're not talking about Mr. Faint over here," Rishi joked, motioning at Slim. "We're talking about you . . . about Rodney 'McThugg Slayer' Rathbone."

"Yeah, relax," Dave added.

My friends were right, of course. How could I be foolish enough to worry that one little yelp would tarnish my golden reputation? I'd be fine. I actually smiled for the first time since Saturday as I walked into the cafeteria to line up for class.

"Aaaaggghhhhhh!" A scream rang out so loud that I jumped and froze. It was Kayla, pointing in my direction as she held her stomach and bent over laughing. Samantha was right beside her, practically crying from howling.

"Please stop this at once," Long Nose pleaded with the girls, but they seemed determined to have fun, all at my expense.

"Any mutants grab you this morning, Rodney?" Kayla yelled.

Samantha joined in, "Did you spill your cereal all over the place and run to Mommy?" They both began giggling uncontrollably. I made a face like they were crazy but noticed other kids starting to look in my direction and laugh along with the girls. Then I saw Jessica, who wasn't laughing. She was too busy listening to Mr. California, who was smirking as he whispered something in her ear.

If things had ended with that, I would have been miserable but safe. However, someone else was listening and his curiosity was aroused. Toby went over and sat right next to the girls. I could see him ask them something and the two girls launched into giggly whispers, no doubt describing the whole embarrassing scene. Toby was salivating, his devilish eyes gleaming right at me. This wasn't going away anytime soon.

I was miserable all morning. It didn't help matters seeing Toby enjoy himself so much. As Mrs. Lutzkraut droned on, he kept busy sketching ugly mutants eating screaming stick figures. Each figure wore a little T-shirt with the name Rodney on it. For my viewing pleasure, he made sure to place the drawings where I could see them, his lips locked in a smile the whole time.

Lunch arrived and I sat down with my friends. They seemed completely clueless about my various problems. As they joked about something from class, I nervously watched the rest of the cafeteria. All my fears were being realized. Kayla and Samantha were still making mutant faces at me from the next table and squealing with delight. Greg sat down next to Jessica and I almost pounded my sandwich into a pancake when he began feeding her his Cool Ranch Doritos. I watched for several seconds, growing nauseous and believing things couldn't get any worse. Then I looked to my right. Boy, was I was wrong.

At the other end of my table sat Toby and Josh. I could tell they had been waiting to make eye contact. I gulped. Josh hadn't given me such a direct, threatening look since the first day of school. He mouthed the words, "You're dead."

"Don't you just love lunchtime?" Rishi elbowed me.

"Uh . . ."

"I can't wait to get outside and play some b-ball."

Oh no, recess. That's where Josh would probably get me. I wanted no part of it. There was no way I was going outside. "Well, have fun," I told Rishi.

"Huh? Where you going?"

"See you in half an hour," I said as I got up to leave.

"But Rodney," I could hear him begin as I walked away. I had to get past Long Nose. After that, I would come up with a plan. I kept my head down and walked toward the door.

"Just where do you think you're going?" she asked.

"I'm sitting out recess with Mrs. Lutzkraut," I answered out of habit.

Her squinty eyes dug deep into mine. I was sure she could tell I was lying. "Excellent," she finally announced, "but if *I* was a teacher, you would *really* know what punishment is all about. None of this silly missing recess stuff. If I had my way, you would have been expelled a long time ago. And do you know what else?" She motioned for me to come closer, like she had a secret.

I took a step forward. She slowly bent over me—and blew her whistle so loud that I fell backward. "Line up time!" she shouted to the cafeteria.

As I walked through the doors and down the long gray hallway, my ears still ringing, I could hear her screeching at everyone to head outdoors. I was glad to be out of there and for a minute considered hiding in the bathroom, or talking to Mr. Feebletop about the latest Mets trade. Instead, though, I headed straight to room 217. I walked in and for the first time ever was actually relieved to see Mrs. Lutzkraut at her desk.

"What are *you* doing here?" she muttered angrily, a glob of egg salad falling from her mouth.

I almost gagged but managed to answer, "You told me to come today." Then I added, "Tomorrow, too." She looked slightly confused and frowned. I figured this would be the best place for me to hide for a while.

Mrs. Lutzkraut seemed as disgusted to see me as I was to see that slimy food churning in her mouth. She finally spoke. "I don't remember telling you to come here. Knowing you, you're probably wrong, but no doubt you deserve to be sitting out recess anyway. Take a seat, and for once be quiet."

My quick thinking had worked. As bored and grossed out as I was sitting out recess in class, at least I was safe. But for how long? What would I do after tomorrow? I slipped into such a down mood that Mrs. Lutzkraut seemed baffled by my silence. Right before the rest of the kids returned to class she looked at me and announced, "I know I'll regret this, but you behaved so well today that I've had a change of heart. Rodney, tomorrow you may join your friends outside for recess."

Chapter 20

NO PAIN, NO GAIN

I was still moping about when my mom called me to dinner that evening. I sat looking at my plate of lasagna. Normally I would have inhaled it, but tonight I just flicked my fork between the layers and pushed the ricotta cheese around the plate. "Are you feeling okay?" my mom asked.

"Yeah, I guess. Well, not really." My mom put down her fork and felt my forehead. "I'm not sick, Mom. I just had a bad day. Can I go to private school?"

"No, too expensive," my dad commented, his mouth half full. He broke off a piece of bread and wiped his plate clean. Sometimes he ate faster than a dog.

"What happened today?" my mom asked. My sister was watching me now and even my dad looked concerned . . . until I realized he was eyeing my lasagna.

"It's a long story, but if I come home tomorrow missing a few teeth, don't be surprised." I felt my eyes start to get a little watery. It was both torturous and a relief to be talking about my problems with someone other than a weird old guy in a haunted house.

"I thought you took care of that problem," my dad said.

"I guess my good luck ran out. I'm dead tomorrow." I glanced around the table. My mom looked concerned, my dad scratched his chin thinking, and Penny was smiling widely.

"No, you're not!" my mom insisted. "I'm calling the school first thing in the morning. Mrs. Lutzkraut will . . ."

"Hold on, there," my dad chimed in. "That won't solve anything. It'll just make matters worse."

"Donald, I'm not going to let some school ruffians hurt my darling angel. I . . ."

"Princess, will let *me* handle this. No boy wants his mom calling the school. Am I right, Rodney?"

"Uh, well . . ."

"You see, dear. Besides, Rodney has nothing to worry about. I have a surefire plan. Now, if you're done," he announced, reaching for my plate, "you can leave the table."

"Donald Rathbone!" my mother snapped, grabbing the plate in midair and returning it to my place. "I hope your great scheme works better than your attempt to steal Rodney's dinner."

A little later I joined my dad in the den. My sister hovered by the door, eager to see what was going to happen. I was curious too. "Hit me in the stomach," my dad began.

"What?"

"Hit me in the stomach. Throw your best punch."

Great, I thought. Here comes that lasagna dinner he just wolfed down. I made a fist anyway.

"No, no. Let me see that hand." My dad took my fist and examined it. "The only thing you're going to break with that is your thumb. Keep your thumb on the *outside* of your knuckles." As he spoke, he positioned my thumb where he wanted it. "There. That's better."

"Now, the next thing is knowing where to punch. You proved you know how to hit someone in the nose, but it's not always easy to punch someone's face, particularly if he's bigger than you. It can be hard to reach. It's better to hit the body. Do you know where to aim?"

"The stomach?"

"No, there's somewhere better."

"I thought you weren't allowed to punch someone there. . . ."

"Not *there*," my dad continued. "Look, see this doll?" He grabbed one of Penny's dolls with his left hand and held it up by the neck. "See the middle of the chest? That's the solar plexus. A good hit there will put anyone down. Knock the wind right out of them. Watch closely. Pow!" And with that he punched the doll in the gut, sending the body flying halfway across the room. The doll's head, still in my dad's grip, stared straight ahead.

"Kiiiiitttttttttttt!" Penny shrieked. "Mommy, Mommy!

Daddy killed my American Girl doll!" My father dropped Kit's head as my mom entered the den.

"Sorry, dear, I got carried away," he explained.

"I don't like this whole thing. Teaching Rodney how to fight . . ."

"Sweetie, this is self-defense, it's like that Pilates stuff you do down at the gym. . . ."

"Pilates has nothing to do with . . ."

"Honey, we're almost done. Oh, and one more thing. Rodney and I are going to watch *Rocky III* tonight if you want to join us." My mom just groaned as she grabbed my crying sister and left the room.

As we sat there watching the movie, my dad and I practiced sparring. He had me throwing punch combinations while repeating different fight-inspired expressions. "Pop, pop, bang. No pain, no gain. 'Eye of the Tiger'!" By the time Rocky and Apollo Creed were training to beat 'Clubber' Lang, I almost felt ready to fight Josh. The movie ended and my dad said, "In the first movie, Rocky had to chase a chicken around. I wonder where I could get a live chicken. . . ."

Even though I was tired from staying up late, I couldn't sleep that night. I kept making a fist and throwing jabs at the ceiling, wondering if I really had what it takes.

I awoke in a somber mood that didn't fade as the day wore on. I didn't laugh at my friends' jokes on the bus, and when Josh climbed aboard and started to make a face at me, I didn't flinch. I was ready. I kept my eyes locked on his and for a fleeting second his face looked a little less confident. Then his eyes hardened again. We both knew it was on.

I didn't say a word in class. I squeezed my fists, visualizing the upcoming showdown. Not once did I look at Jessica. I didn't eat my ham sandwich at lunch. I looked ahead, concentrating on uppercuts and jabs. If Rishi, Slim, and Dave noticed my mood they didn't say anything; or maybe they did and I didn't notice.

Eventually the whistle blew and we stood to go outside. Almost through a fog, I could hear Long Nose screaming at some kids to clean up their table. I shuffled along with the rest of the students toward the door and before I knew it I was out in the fresh air. I breathed in deeply. My head seemed to clear. I noticed all my surroundings and the faces of other students. My awareness was heightened and everything became sharpened. And more than anything else, my brain screamed, *Get the heck out of here!*

The old panic was setting in. "Eye of the Tiger"? All I wanted to do was run like a chicken. I kept my head down and moved closer toward the aides, where Long Nose stood ranting about student behavior. I figured maybe I'd be safe near them. Seeing me, she snapped, "What do you want?"

"I, uh, I was just, uh . . ." I stammered.

"Well you can just 'uh' somewhere else. Go on, get

going." She stared at me until I moved away. No help from the adults. I headed toward some trees where I could possibly hide for a while. As I crossed the basketball court, my friends caught up with me. "Where you going?" Slim asked. "We've been looking all over for you. Do you want to play basketball or kickball?"

"Looks like he wants to play Hide-and-Seek."

Too late. I was found. Toby stood there smiling as Josh approached from the far end of the court like a shark that smelled blood. My blood.

I didn't run. My dad's boxing quotes from last night raced through my mind: *No pain, no gain. Stay off the ropes. Stick and move. Duck and weave. Float like a butterfly and sting like a bee.* I realized I had no clue what any of them meant, and my knees started to wobble. Toby was smiling, anticipating the moment he'd been dreaming about the whole school year. Josh, on the other hand, didn't smile. He looked perfectly evil. His eyes were dark and determined, his fists ready to pulverize some meat.

My friends shifted behind me. Rishi nodded and said, "Looks like it's time you gave those two punks another lesson."

Yes, on how to run, I thought.

"All right, Rathbone, time for you to taste my knuckles." Josh loomed right before me, glaring.

"Yeah and . . ." Toby began to chime in, but Josh interrupted him.

"No more talk, Toby! Time to die, Rathbone." At that, his body charged, meeting mine. I would have been knocked down like a palm tree in a hurricane but I fell back into Slim's belly and bounced forward into Josh's chest, my clenched fist connecting with his solar panel, or whatever my dad had called it. I could hear a hollow thud and Josh wheezed, startled. My friends erupted into howls, until a piercing scream rang out louder than all of them. Louder than anything I'd ever heard before. We all turned and saw it was coming from Long Nose, who was clutching her head as a basketball slowly bounced to a stop in back of her.

The entire playground was silent, except for Long Nose. Josh had lowered his fists and was watching the scene like the rest of us. Long Nose held the back of her head in her hands, moaning and cursing. Her eyes were teary and red. The other aides huddled around, touching her shoulders and hair. Suddenly she flung their hands off and stormed toward the court.

Most of the kids slunk away, except for Jessica and Greg, who stood there in shock. One of them had thrown the ball, I realized. Long Nose must have assumed the same thing, for she headed their way. I also paid attention to Josh. He was still absorbed in the drama.

"Who threw the basketball?" Long Nose demanded. Greg was closest to her and tried to back away. "You, tan boy. Did you throw it at me?"

"No," Greg nervously squeaked.

"No? Then who did?"

He was stumbling, beginning to panic. I knew all the signs intimately.

"Tell me who?" Long Nose screamed at him. He jerked his head at Jessica.

Long Nose swung toward her with a face contorted by rage. It looked like she might grab Jessica and shake her. "So it was *you*, my little pretty! You threw it at me?" Jessica's lips were quivering and she was unable to utter a sound.

"Speak up!" Long Nose screamed into Jessica's face.

"*I* threw it!" I shouted, seeing a way to escape Josh's beating.

"Now you're going to get it," Rishi whispered.

Long Nose wheeled my way. "Rodney! I should have known. You are nothing but trouble. *With a capital* ***T****!* You are going to wish you never came to this school. We're going straight to Mr. Feebletop and I'll make sure you never see recess again. Expulsion is too good for you. I will personally see that your time at Baber is a living . . ."

Still ranting like a lunatic, she gave my shoulder a not-so-tender squeeze and off we went. She continued ranting through all the halls until we arrived at Mr. Feebletop's office, where she barged right in, me in tow.

Mr. Feebletop looked up from his turkey sandwich. He reached back, turned off what sounded like sports talk radio, chewed the bite in his mouth, and looked questioningly at Long Nose. She exhaled and in an upset tone asked, "Mr. Feebletop, do you know what this boy did today at recess?"

Mr. Feebletop glanced at me for the first time. He practically spit out his bite. "Rodney, did you hear who the Mets got?" Before I could answer, I felt Long Nose's fingertips dig deeper into my shoulder. Mr. Feebletop must have also felt her silent, annoyed presence, for he collected himself and asked, "Mrs. Whiner, please explain to me what happened."

Mrs. Whiner? It had never occurred to me that Long Nose had a real name.

She let go of my shoulder and brought her hand to her chest. "Well, this boy threw a basketball and it hit me in the back of the head. It almost knocked me out. I have quite a headache." She was laying it on thick.

Mr. Feebletop grunted, then looked at me. "Rodney, you know a basketball is a very heavy ball. Did you mean to throw it?"

"No, Mr. Feebletop. I think I was fouled as I took a shot." I had expected him to ask this.

"Did you, or any of the other aides, see the shot?" Mr. Feebletop asked Long Nose.

"Well, no, but, well, it sure hurt."

Mr. Feebletop looked down at his sandwich and thought for a moment. I wasn't sure if he was thinking about what to do with me or whether to take another bite. Finally he leaned back. "It certainly sounds like an accident, so I think what we'll do is . . . hmm . . . yes, I know. Rodney, no basketball for a week."

Long Nose looked like a kettle about to blow. I cringed in anticipation. "Mr. Feebletop! This boy assaulted me. I don't think you understand the pain he caused me. I think his punishment should be significant. He's a danger to everyone."

Mr. Feebletop looked back at his sandwich. It didn't seem to provide him much comfort, for he sighed and replied, "I understand that you are in pain. Go see the nurse right after you leave. I'll tell you what. I'll have Rodney spend recess tomorrow here in the office, but Thursday he can go back outside, and no basketball for the month, Rodney. I think that's a logical and fair solu—"

Long Nose interrupted. "I don't think you understand. Either he receives a punishment that befits such a horrid act, or I quit!" She swept her hand across her body in a dramatic gesture of good-bye. It was her greatest mistake. Her hand clipped the top of Mr. Feebletop's prize Tom Seaver baseball, causing it to shoot past the principal's grasp and bounce once on his desk before landing in the garbage pail. Mr. Feebletop jumped up and peered in. "Tom!"

I craned my neck to see around the side of the desk as he retrieved it. Coffee and coffee grinds covered the baseball. He tried frantically to blot it with a napkin, but it was too late. The signature was already smeared. For a few seconds he looked at it with a forlorn expression. Then the sadness in his face left and was replaced by a quiet seriousness I'd never seen in him before. He looked at me and said, "Rodney, you can return to recess. We will finish discussing this later."

I got up out of my chair and left his office. I saw that the secretaries weren't there, and my curiosity got the better of me. Acting like my little snoop of a sister, I lingered by the door and listened in.

Mr. Feebletop cleared his throat. "I accept your resignation."

"What?" she screamed.

"A moment ago you said you were planning to quit, so you can go now," he added. I was in shock.

Long Nose sounded like she was hyperventilating. She seemed on the verge of screaming or crying and wound up doing both. I figured it was time to leave before she stormed out of the office. The last thing I heard was Mr. Feebletop mutter, "He signed it on my birthday, too."

The other aides were lining up the students to go back in when I returned to recess. My smiling face brought a lot of attention and excitement. It was as if a wave swept through the grade. I saw right away that Rishi, Slim, Dave, Jessica, Kayla, Josh, Toby, and maybe thirty others were waiting to see what had happened. They started to approach me.

My return, however, was immediately interrupted and overshadowed by Long Nose, who burst through the door and came running outside with her arms swinging over her head. She was still teary and frantic. Seeing me, she flinched and uttered a strange, crazy sound like a cat whose tail has just gotten crunched by a rocking chair. "Ohaahaaaahah! I will get you for this, Rodney!" Still yelling and waving her hands around, she ran to the parking lot and stumbled. One of her high heels fell off and for a second she tried to put it back on but was too hysterical. Instead she threw it at us, screaming, "Rotten kids!" She jumped into her red car, gunned it, and with tires screeching zoomed out of our lives.

The whole crowd stood in astonishment, students and aides alike. Josh was staring at me with a questioning look on his face. That's when I saw Toby shove him in the shoulder and say, "Get him." Josh whirled around, flattened Toby with a hard shove, and stomped off to his teacher's line. Apparently, the Long Nose mystery was enough to convince Josh that my powers weren't something to mess with. I wasn't sure how long Josh would be off my back, but for now I had escaped! Again!

Rishi was the first to come up to me. "I don't know how you do it, but you're brilliant. Jessica's been crying for you for twenty minutes, plus you got rid of Long Nose. Are you like some superhero or something? Do you have mind-control powers? Hey, if you do, can you get Lutzkraut to give me an *A* in math?" I laughed and he was already pretending to be a version of me with superpowers. "Slim, with my mind-control powers, I demand you kiss Mrs. Lutzkraut."

He held up his hands and wiggled his fingers at Slim, who scrunched up his lips and said, "Mmmm, Lutzkraut, pretty." He did his best zombie imitation.

I may have joined in the goofing around, but through the crowd I noticed someone looking at me with full interest. As students wandered over to listen to Rishi's goofs, Jessica came up to me and asked, "Rodney, how could you be so noble?" I think she wanted to say a lot more, but Greg had come over to join us.

"Uh, Jessica," he began. Before he could say another word Kayla was all over him.

"Way to go, Robin Hood. Nice way to protect your princess!" She continued hammering Greg, who eventually muttered something about needing to get back in line. Jessica looked at me and was about to open her mouth when we were interrupted again. Mrs. Lutzkraut had appeared to take us back to class.

"Jessica and Rodney, in line. Rishi and Kayla, zip it. Toby, brush off your pants. And Timothy, stop scrunching your lips at me." Recess was definitely over, but I didn't care. I was floating the rest of the day.

Chapter 21

ROCCO RONBONI

In the days and weeks following the dismissal of Long Nose, most kids were in awe of me. They kept asking about what happened in Feebletop's office that could have made Long Nose lose it like that. I got good at keeping them guessing. Even with Rishi and my closest friends, I would just say, "Hey, us New Yorkers know how to get things done." If they wondered how I really did it, or secretly feared I did something awful, they didn't mention it. They were too busy enjoying themselves. Lunch and recess were much more pleasant when you didn't get yelled at and made to stand in line.

The fact that I might be capable of black magic cast just the right spell when it came to Josh. Although I knew that every part of him wanted to use my face for a punching bag, he stayed away. Maybe he was afraid I'd turn him into a toad.

Even better, ever since I rescued her from Long Nose, Jessica and I were spending lots of time together. I was still trying to get up the nerve to formally ask her out, but things were good. And as for Greg, well, he never regained Jessica's attention, although he got plenty of it from Kayla. "Did you wet your pants today on the basketball court, Greg? What's the matter? Do you want Jessica to protect you?" Poor Greg. He had no comebacks, and his popularity eventually faded . . . along with his tan. He was so pathetic that I even forgave him and wound up including him in my group of friends.

Yes, in the weeks after Long Nose left, things were just how I liked them. There were even brief moments when I believed things were as good as they seemed, but try as I might to be happy and content, there was a black cloud on the horizon. Its name was Rocco Ronboni, and it was about to rain down hard on me.

I knew what was coming before my mother even told me. It was that look on her face—a happy, excited look that usually spelled disaster for me. I could feel the hairs rising on the back of my neck. Penny sensed it too and perked up in her chair. My dad just kept shoveling french fries into his mouth.

"Donald, you're going to choke," my mom commented.

"*Hugfgsj*," he replied with a full mouth.

"Can you slow down for a moment? I want to make an . . ."

"When do they get here?" I said, standing up from the table.

My mom looked confused, then she giggled. "I don't know how you knew it, but the Ronbonis are flying in tonight! I'm showing them around town tomorrow. Rocco is visiting school the day after tomorrow and . . ."

"I need to be excused," I interrupted.

"What about your dinner?" my mom asked.

I didn't answer or stick around to hear any more good news. If Rocco beat me up at school, everything in my life would go from great to rotten in about two minutes. I had to come up with a plan. Actually, for two months I had been trying to come up with a plan, only I kept drawing blanks. Now there was no time left.

I went into my room and sat down on the bed. "Think!" I commanded myself. For the next hour or so, a steady stream of plans entered my head—each one dumber than the next. I could buy a costume and disguise myself. I could rob a bank and bribe Rocco with millions of dollars. I could dig an escape tunnel under Baber Intermediate. . . .

"You're scared about Rocco, right?" My sister was standing in the doorway. She was the only other person in the entire state of Ohio who knew about my beatings back in New York.

"What? Me scared? I'm sure you've heard at school how I'm like the toughest . . ."

"Rodney, I don't know how you've been tricking

everyone, but I know you're afraid of Rocco coming."

I couldn't tell if she wanted to help me or if she was about to start gloating, but I didn't want to take a chance.

"Okay, out of here!" I jumped up off the bed. "The last thing I need is my little sister . . ."

"If you're not there, he can't do anything."

My hand was on her back, pushing her out into the hallway. I stopped. "What is that supposed to mean?"

"I mean, if you're not there, Rocco can't do anything to you. You should just disappear for the day."

"What do you want me to do? Drink a magic potion that will make me invisible? Penny, go watch TV. . . ."

I shoved her out the door and flung myself onto the bed, my sister's silly words echoing in my head. "If you're not there, he can't do anything." *What a dopey idea,* I thought.

Or was it? Maybe Penny was on to something.

Rocco was only visiting Baber for one day before heading back to New York. If I wasn't in school that day, what could he do? Even if he told everyone stuff about New York, no one would believe him.

But where could I hide for a whole day? The mall? Someone would report me. The library? Same problem. I settled into the pillow and closed my eyes. I figured I'd worry about it tomorrow. After all, I wouldn't be seeing Rocco for another two days. At least, that's what I thought.

• • •

The next day at school I tried to act as normal as I could, but it was tough. I had a hard time joking with my friends or annoying Mrs. Lutzkraut. I still didn't know what I would do when Rocco showed up. The more I thought about it, though, the more I liked the idea of hiding. First of all, we were supposed to be reading out loud in class the next day and I was dreading that. In fact, probably because I was so worried about everything, I actually told Jessica about my fear of reading or speaking in front of a group. She laughed and told me I would do fine, which made me feel better, but that still left my other problem.

As the day wore on, I made the decision to definitely spend the next day in hiding. Sure, I'd probably get into trouble. The school would call home, my parents would be mad, but that would be far better than a visit from Rocco. Only one question remained—where to hide?

My brain finally sharpened when I climbed off the bus in the afternoon. I had always noticed a path that led off from the bus stop into some thick woods. That's it. I could spend tomorrow in those woods instead of getting on the bus. I would already have my lunch with me. . . .

"Rodney, what are you thinking about? You seem out of it," Rishi said.

He was looking off into the trees trying to figure out what had grabbed my attention.

I wasn't about to confide in him. "Oh, nothing much. Let's go home."

Together we walked along the sidewalk. The streets were empty and the air was still. We were approaching a three-way intersection down the street from my house. Suddenly, something felt wrong.

"Well, look who's coming," Rishi said, smiling. I glanced down Clark Street and frowned. Josh and Toby were trudging along with their heads down. Toby looked up and the two of them stopped about fifteen yards from us. This was a potentially dangerous moment and sweat began to run down my rubbery spine.

"Who's that?" Rishi asked.

"Josh and Toby. Did you go blind?"

"Not them. Over *there*."

My eyes turned from Clark Street and looked down the third street that met the intersection. I grabbed Rishi's arm to keep from falling to the pavement. I couldn't believe it, but there he was. Rocco Ronboni. He looked meaner than I remembered and bigger, too.

He was shuffling along with his patented strut. A silver NYC flashed on his black sweatshirt and his hair stood straight up on his head like a black porcupine. Seeing me, he stopped walking and gave me a wicked grin.

And there we stood, all five of us. A breeze blew and the sweat on my back ran cold. My eyes shifted from Rocco to Josh and Toby and then back to Rocco.

"Yo, Ratboy. Ya miss me?" Rocco called and walked toward me. "Been lookin' all over for yuh." Josh and Toby, their evil noses smelling potential violence, strode up too.

My mouth stammered, "Uh yeah, I thought you were coming tomorrow, though. I was going to throw you a surprise welcome party. In fact, why don't you turn around and run along. Try to act surprised tomorrow."

"That mouth of yours still runnin', huh? So dis is Ohio? Smells bad, like da country. I miss New York already." Rocco looked over at Josh and Toby. He paused for a moment, taking in Josh's size. "Dees yuh friends?" he asked me.

"We ain't friends," Toby spat.

"No doubt," Rocco laughed, adding, "I like da looks of yous two. I betcha yous been handing Rodney some beatdowns. But don't worry. I'm movin' into this town, and poundin' dis kid is *my* job." Josh looked confused by this, but Toby's eyes shone as he listened.

Rishi spoke next, and the second he opened his mouth I knew we were in trouble. "Are you like the dumbest kid in New York?" he asked. "No one messes with Rodney Rathbone and gets away with it."

Boy, is he going to be disappointed in a minute, I thought.

Rocco shifted quickly and got into Rishi's space. "Dat's gotta be the funniest thing I ever hoyed. And now, afta I'm done smackin' him around for old times' sake, I'm gonna give you a liddle taste of da Big Apple." He smiled and looked back over at Josh and Toby. Toby was smiling, enjoying every second of this. Josh just looked confused.

Rishi wasn't done, though. "Like I'm supposed to be

scared. I almost feel bad for you! Rodney's going to tear you apart! Rodney here . . ." he gripped my shoulder for effect.

"Rishi, quiet," I whispered.

". . . well, Rodney took out four grown men with his bare hands. And do you know what else he did?"

"Not now, Rishi," I whispered. I felt real bad knowing what was coming. After watching his supertough friend get beaten up, Rishi would be next. Unaware that he was digging his grave deeper, he kept right on talking.

"The first day of school, Rodney punched out *that* guy!" Rishi's finger pointed at Josh.

"Awright, now I've hoyed it awl! Dis is one wacky town." Rocco laughed and strutted toward Josh. "Rodney knocked you out?"

"I broke his nose, too," I added, trying to get the attention off Rishi.

"Really?" Rocco laughed even harder and slapped his knee. Josh stiffened, but didn't answer.

Once Rocco gained control of himself, he looked Josh in the eye. Although Rocco was real big, even he had to glance upward to meet Josh's gaze. "Who are you?" Rocco continued, "the town's big-boy cream puff? You let *him* beat you up? You gotta be the biggest wimp I've ever seen. What's your name? Nawww wait, let me guess. Is it Jennifer? Or Marcy? Or . . ."

Rocco didn't get a chance to think of any other girls'

names. Josh grabbed him with both arms and hoisted him up in the air.

Rocco's face looked shocked. He struggled but couldn't escape from Josh's mammoth hands.

"Ooh, this should be good," Rishi gasped, taking out his camera.

"Put me down!" Rocco screamed.

Josh said, "Sure." Walking closer to the curb, he body-slammed Rocco into some garbage cans.

Toby, ever helpful in these situations, said, "Welcome to Ohio," and dumped garbage from another can onto the visiting tough guy. Rocco eventually scrambled up and ran, crying, down the block while Rishi's camera clicked away.

Josh and Toby high-fived each other, and I almost joined them, but Rocco had said a lot and I wasn't in the clear just yet.

The four of us straightened up and squared off. Josh spoke first. "That wimp, he said he used to beat you up. That true?"

"Yeah, right," Rishi jumped in. "That kid's obviously got some mental . . ."

"I ain't talking to you. Rathbone, is it true what that kid said?"

Now, I knew I had only one chance. I rolled my head back and forth and cracked my knuckles. "Why don't you come over here and find out?" Other than the shaking knees and a sudden urge to wet my pants, the bluff seemed convincing.

"Yeah," Rishi added. "Why don't you go over to Rodney and find out!"

Oh great.

"Rodney's not afraid of anything or anyone!"

Shut up.

Josh stood there thinking, which looked difficult for him. Toby nudged him on, but he shoved Toby off. "Okay. That was enough for one day. Come on, Tobe."

They walked on by. I could see Toby's disappointment. Once they had gone a block, I exhaled slowly through my teeth.

"Well, that was fun," Rishi said, punching my arm. "Let's go get a snack."

We headed back to my house. Penny, who was watching her after-school shows on TV, actually put it on MUTE when she saw us. That was a first.

"Did Rocco find you?" she asked. "He stopped here before. He was looking for you."

"Yeah, he found me," I told her. "No big deal."

She looked surprised. "Really?"

"Really."

Rishi joined the conversation. "And you should have seen Rodney scare off Josh!"

Now Penny looked really confused. "I don't get it. . . ."

"That's because you're still young," I teased her. "Come on, Rishi. Let's hit the kitchen."

• • •

That night, before going to bed, I made a decision. No hiding for me the next day. I didn't want to miss seeing Josh teach Rocco another lesson, but that was only part of it. Suddenly hiding in the woods seemed kind of dumb, like something you would do if you were . . . well . . . a coward.

Chapter 22

A WORM IN THE BIG APPLE

Rocco never showed up at school the next day. It turns out his mother was outraged by how the local kids had treated her little angel. After months of worry, Rocco wasn't moving. Maybe everything had worked out perfectly for me. Even my fear of reading in front of the class was for nothing. Mrs. Lutzkraut was out sick for a few days, and by the time she came back we had moved on to other class work.

It was around this time that I finally came to think of Garrettsville as my new true home. Sure, I still missed different things about New York, but one day coming home from school I walked up the steps to my house and accepted the fact that I really belonged here. There was no going back.

"Guess what?" my mom greeted me. "You're going back!"

"To school?" I didn't know what she was talking about.

"No. To New York! Isn't that great news?"

In a flash, I pictured Jessica, Rishi, my other friends, and how popular I was at Baber. I had solved every problem. No way was I going back. There was nothing my parents could do. If we were moving again, I'd chain myself to a tree. . . .

"Your birthday's coming up. Aunt Evelyn has invited you to New York as her guest this weekend to celebrate it."

"Just for the weekend? Aunt Evelyn?" A flood of relief washed over me. Every spring Aunt Evelyn would take me into the city for my birthday. She would also take Penny for hers, but that wasn't until August. Now that we lived in Ohio, I had an important question for my mom. "Uh, how am I going to get there for the weekend?"

"You'll fly."

"By myself?" The old familiar feeling of panic crept up my spine.

"Yes. After I got off the phone with her I called the airline and they have a program for unaccompanied minors. Dad will drop you off Friday morning and she'll meet you when you land in New York. You'll have to miss a day of school, of course."

The whole thing sounded a bit crazy. I wasn't thrilled about flying by myself, but I liked the idea of missing a day with Lutzkraut. More important, a whole weekend with my aunt Evelyn could mean only one thing—adventure!

• • •

I couldn't wait for Friday, and before I knew it the day had arrived. My dad saw me off at the airport. He handed me a cell phone and told me to call when I landed.

Two hours later I was back on New York soil. I made my way down the long airport corridor. Just as I was stumbling off a moving sidewalk, I heard loud music playing up ahead. I continued on, trying to see past the other travelers and get a glimpse of the commotion.

And then I saw her, Aunt Evelyn, waiting for me with what must have been 100 balloons. I ran up to her and gave her a hug.

"You got all those balloons for me?" I asked, shocked.

"Yes, sorry it's a bit underwhelming. Airport security refused to let the Mariachi band through the checkpoint."

"Aunt Evelyn, you didn't have to do that!"

"Nonsense. It's not every day my favorite nephew visits. Now come here and give me a kiss."

As we walked through the airport she told me how "ecstatic" and "tickled" she was to see me. She also told me about her latest trip and kept mentioning places like Cape Town, Ulaanbaatar, and Bogotá. "By the way, how was your flight?" she eventually asked.

"Terrible," I told her. "I'm starving. Dad ate my lunch on the way to the airport and they didn't serve any food. I couldn't even have peanuts because the guy next to me was allergic."

We grabbed my suitcase off the baggage carousel and headed out into the warm spring day. My great-aunt whistled to a passing cab and it immediately screeched to a halt, then backed up to right where we were standing. "Let's go have some fun!" she shouted as we hopped in the back.

"Do you think we could hit McDonald's first?"

"McDonald's? Driver, take us to Fifty-fifth and Seventh and make it snappy!" She turned back to me. "I can't have my darling nephew hungry."

A half hour later I was sitting in the Carnegie Deli eating a pastrami sandwich the size of a Cadillac. I could barely fit it into my mouth. My aunt fed me and fed me and when we were done, she rolled me out the door onto Seventh Avenue. "Rodney," she said, "you'll have to help me get ready. I'm hosting a dinner party tonight. Let's walk over to the park and make plans."

I watched the crowds of people moving through the streets and smelled the heavy, sweet New York City air. I had forgotten how much I loved it. Aunt Evelyn was as excited as ever by life, the whole time talking about who was coming to her dinner and what fun things we could do the rest of the weekend. Suddenly she waved to someone in a restaurant window as we passed. He waved back and threw her a kiss.

"How do you know so many people?" I asked.

"My darling boy, I've lived in this town for practically a hundred years."

I knew she was exaggerating, but I wasn't sure by how much.

"Now, where was I?" she continued. "Oh yes, I've only been back for two days myself. I'd love to see the new Picasso exhibit this afternoon at the Guggenheim, maybe a play Saturday night, of course there's our annual birthday ballgame tomorrow at one o'clock. I *did* tell you we were seeing the Mets tomorrow, didn't I?"

Before I could answer, she was off on some other subject. She was full of energy and interested in everything. That afternoon, my great-aunt and I visited two museums and took a brisk stroll down Fifth Avenue. When we finally got back to her apartment, I put my feet up and wondered how I'd last the whole weekend. As long as I was resting, I decided to give Rishi a call.

"I'm telling you, New York is wild. My aunt Evelyn snuck her Rollerblades into this round museum called the Guggenheim and zoomed all the way down from the top floor. She finally crashed at the bottom into a famous statue by this guy named Rodin."

"Rodent? Who'd want to see that?" Rishi and I laughed and talked for a while more before his mother told him to hang up and get ready for dinner.

"Listen, Rodney, call me tomorrow," he whispered. "Also, check your e-mail when you get a chance. I sent you some funny pictures of your friend Rocco. Oh, and I've got some big news for you."

Before I could find out the news, he was gone. I

thought about calling Dave or Slim when the intercom in my aunt's apartment started buzzing. For the next half hour, my aunt's friends kept arriving for the dinner party, each one dressed funnier and fancier than the next. They were all supernice and I liked them a lot. That is, until Sir Snottingham showed up.

He walked in and I immediately noticed his long white mustache which curled upward at the corners of his mouth. He was wearing a heavy black overcoat and clutching a cane, which he clicked hard on the wood floor. Noticing me, he whipped off his coat and tossed it over my head as if I was a coatrack. I heard him say, "Careful with that. It's cashmere." I pulled it off, and for a second we studied each other. "Stop gawking, boy. Aren't you going to announce me?"

"Who are you?"

He stiffened and asked, "Are you trying to be rude or does it just come naturally? I find it hard to believe that anyone would need to ask that question. I happen to be the most important person at this party."

I felt my mouth getting ready. "Well, why didn't you say so?" I turned and yelled into the living room. "Aunt Evelyn, the caterer's here!"

"*Caterer?* You call me the caterer? Why I've had boys younger than you arrested for less. I . . ."

"Oh, Sir Edward, I'm so happy you could make it. I see you've met my nephew," Aunt Evelyn said as she came toward us.

He seemed momentarily at a loss, and then managed, "What's that? Your nephew? Oh, I see. Yes, we've, uh, met."

"Rodney, this is Sir Edward Snottingham, former conductor of the Royal Symphony Orchestra in England."

I reached out to shake his hand. Instead, he dropped his cane into my palm. "Put that with the coat," he quipped. He turned his back on me and grabbed my aunt's arm. I dumped his coat and cane on the floor.

Sir Snottingham aside, my aunt's friends were great. Unfortunately, he made sure he was seated right next to my aunt and spent half the dinner trying to sound important, especially about concerts and Broadway shows and stuff.

"Oh Evelyn, please tell me you're joking. How could you *not* have seen the new *Death of a Salesman*? Victor Johnson is truly excellent."

"You know I've been out of town, darling."

"Oh, too bad, Evelyn, he's in it for only one more night. It would be the highlight of the season if we shared the experience together."

I pretended to stick a finger down my throat. While old Snottingham looked like he wanted to kill me, I could see my aunt holding back a smile.

"Then it's settled, Evelyn," he continued, shooting me a smug little glare. "I will get us two tickets."

"Of course, we'll need three," she pointed out.

"Three?"

"For you, me, and my wonderful nephew here."

I noticed Snottingham pull on the end of his mustache. "Bloody brilliant," he muttered.

The next day, after a whirlwind Manhattan morning that included Rollerblading in Central Park and an early lunch in Harlem, things eventually slowed down when my aunt and I arrived at Citi Field, the Mets' stadium. Orange and blue crowds swarmed around us. We made our way to the right-field gate, my aunt smiling the whole time and saying how much Citi Field reminded her of Ebbets Field, where the Dodgers played when she was young. She then turned to me and asked, "How does it feel to be home, Rodney?"

I don't think she was just talking about the Mets' ball field. She was talking about New York, about Queens, about my old neighborhood. I watched a giant jet fly over on its way into LaGuardia Airport.

"It feels good," I told her.

"Do you miss it?"

"Sometimes, but I like how things are going in Ohio, too."

She looked into my eyes and gave me a big smile. "That makes me very happy, Rodney." Then she snapped out of it. "Let's go see some ball."

We went in and headed toward the field level. *Good sign*, I thought. My dad and I usually rode each and every possible escalator all the way to the very top. I was used to being far away, but I was happier still as we headed through the lower tunnel toward the infield. Even though I'd been to a number of games, I still caught my breath as I came out into the light and air. All the green grass spread out in front of me. It was beautiful. I smelled hot dogs and vendors yelled, "Peanuts here!" We continued walking down the aisle passing rows of seats, getting closer to the field. As I passed each row, my excitement grew, and when we stopped, I found we were in the front row.

"These seats are amazing!" I yelled. We were just beyond the dugout by first base. "How did you get them?"

"Oh, I have a few friends."

And then a voice from the next seat called out, "Evelyn! You made it."

"You know I wouldn't miss it, Tom."

He laughed and came over to join us. The Mets were starting to file out for the bottom of the first.

"I don't believe it. You're Tom Seaver!" I said.

"Most boys your age don't know about me, let alone recognize me," he said and smiled.

"I've spent a lot of time looking at you," I replied.

He raised an eyebrow, and I realized that did sound kind of weird. Aunt Evelyn said, "Tom, this is my nephew, Rodney. Maybe you can autograph a ball or something for him."

I felt like I was in a dream. I'm pretty sure my mouth was hanging open. He nodded and yelled into the dugout. A ball came flying out, which he easily caught. Pulling a permanent marker from a back pocket, he turned to me and asked, "It's Rodney, right?"

"That's right," I heard my aunt answer. The marker approached the ball. . . .

"Wait!" I shouted. Tom Seaver jumped. "Can I tell you what to write?"

He relaxed, smiled, and nodded. "Okay, what'll it be?"

A minute later the first pitch was thrown, a strike, and we all cheered. I turned back to my aunt. "Thanks for getting him to sign the ball for me." I held it in my right hand and kept looking at it.

"Wait until you see the other surprise I cooked up."

Before I had a chance to ask her what that meant, I heard a collective "Rodney!" I turned and coming down the aisle were Timmy, Tony, and Tommy, my three best New York friends.

It was great to see them. After our greetings, we got hot dogs and settled in to watch the game. During the top of the first I described to the three of them how life was going. They laughed a bit when I started talking about Jessica. They had a hard time imagining me as the school tough guy, but they were happy for me.

"Things aren't so hot here," Timmy said. I looked at him and he continued. "Turns out Rocco's not going to move away."

"Really, what did you hear?" I asked him.

Timmy continued. "He came back from that trip not looking too good and was in a real bad mood. He locked Tony in a locker, and said he was here to stay." I felt bad for them, but I breathed a little easier knowing I'd have one less problem in Ohio.

Tommy leaned in so my aunt couldn't hear. "Yesterday he stuck a jockstrap on my head."

Timmy nudged his shoulder. "Don't worry, man, we'll get by. We always have."

I thought for a moment and took out the cell phone my parents had given me for the trip. I fiddled around and brought up Rishi's e-mail. "Perhaps this will help."

"What is it?" all three wondered.

"This is courtesy of my friend, Rishi. I think you'll find he does excellent work."

For the rest of the game they spent as much time looking at the images on my phone as they did watching the action on the field. The Mets lost 4–2, but Timmy, Tony, and Tommy were all smiles.

"I love the one with Rocco buried in garbage," Tommy said.

"Yes, Rishi has an excellent eye," I replied. "I'll send you the whole file."

My aunt and I walked them to the subway and said our good-byes. They were thrilled knowing they now possessed the perfect weapon against Rocco Ronboni—and I was equally thrilled as I gripped the signed baseball. I knew it was going to make someone back at Baber very happy.

I was in such a great mood after the ball game that nothing could get me down—not even hearing Sir Snottingham on my aunt's message machine when we got back from Citi Field:

> *"Evelyn, dear, I'll have you know that I was able to procure us three tickets to tonight's performance. I spoke to my friend who works for the theater, and he said he'd personally put me where I belong. So, my dear Ev, you haven't missed Victor Johnson's last performance. Call me back to arrange where to meet. . . ."*

Several hours later my aunt and I were in a cab pulling up in front of a Broadway theater. I had been to some shows before with her, but this one was different. For starters, it was really packed. Everyone was standing out front dressed real nice, either waiting for other people to arrive or talking in groups. As we stepped out of the cab, Snottingham sauntered over and took my aunt's hand.

"Evelyn, wonderful to see you! Two days in a row. I *am* a lucky man!"

"Oh you," my aunt said, smiling. "Such a gentleman." Meanwhile, Mr. Gentleman only gave me a stern nod before heading off to a window to pick up the tickets.

When he got back, the three of us entered the theater. The whole place was alive with people talking about this Victor Johnson guy and how it was his last performance in the show. I noticed that the usher pointed to the stairs and not the better orchestra section. "No doubt we are in a private box," gloated Sir Snottingham. "Being a conductor has its benefits, you know."

"Former conductor," I corrected him.

He spun around and was about to say something, but just then another usher directed us up more steps to the last row. He snapped, "This is absurd! How dare you stick the conductor of the Royal Symphony Orchestra in the last row!"

"Former conductor," I corrected, and this time I thought I might get cracked with his cane.

"You're not in the last row," the usher pointed out.

A smile of relief flashed over Sir Snottingham's face. "No? Oh, I should have known." He turned down to me and growled, "You see what it's like to be an influential person? Not that you'll ever be one." He straightened back up and addressed the usher. "Now that the little misunderstanding is cleared up, where are we, my good man?"

"You're *behind* the last row. You see those folding chairs in back of that pipe over there?" Snottingham's face turned as red as the theater seats. If his head had exploded, I wouldn't have been shocked. My aunt eventually convinced him it wasn't the end of the world, that partially seeing and partially being able to hear a play were better than nothing. We grabbed little books about the play called Playbills and sat down.

Behind the large pipe, I couldn't see the stage unless I craned my neck all the way to the right. It started to get stiff so I gave up and looked at the Playbill. It was then that I realized I knew the guy on the cover! I couldn't believe it. I looked more closely and it was him! It was Old Man Johnson, from back in Ohio. Of course, Old Man Johnson was an actor from New York. I hoped he would remember me. I turned to my aunt. "I bet I can do something about these seats."

Snottingham laughed. "You? You couldn't even pick your nose correctly."

"Well, you're the expert in that department," I said under my breath.

"Now, now boys," my aunt chimed in before turning to her friend. "This is my nephew we're talking about here." She then reminded me that it was a sold out show and that it would be impossible to do anything.

"Can I at least try?"

My aunt nodded at me with a half smile.

"Bah!" snapped Snottingham. "Go! Don't hurry back."

I walked down the stairs to the front of the orchestra section. No one stopped me in the large theater. The crowd was settling in and buzzing. I went up to an official-looking man at the front of the theater.

"Hi. I was wondering if you'd be able to give my grandfather a message."

"Kid, I'm not your nanny. Find him yourself."

"You'll let me back there to see him?"

"What? What are you going on about?"

"My grandfather, Victor Johnson, can you tell him something for me?"

"You're grandfather is Victor Johnson? Yeah, and I'm Teddy Roosevelt," he laughed.

"Well, Teddy," I said, "I'll tell him later after the show that he didn't get to see his only grandson visiting all the way from Ohio, because you wouldn't give him a little message." I turned to walk away.

"Wait!" He eyed me suspiciously. "Kid, if you're lying to me and I get in trouble for disturbing him, you're going to get it."

"Tell him his grandson, Rodney, from Garrettsville wanted to say hello. Tell him we haven't seen each other since Halloween."

"You better not be playing me," he threatened again and walked off backstage.

Four minutes later he returned followed by Old Man Johnson. "Rodney, so good to see you again. After our little performance, you made the trip. Bravo! You came all this way to see me tonight?" He laughed.

"I didn't know I was seeing you. I looked down at the Playbill and saw your face. It seems impossible," I blurted excitedly.

"Now Rodney, this is Broadway. Nothing is impossible. Where are you sitting?"

"Up behind that pipe. Up there, near the ceiling," I pointed.

"Nonsense! Is the executive box still available?" he asked the usher.

"Yes, but we're saving it. Brad Pitt is supposedly stopping by."

"I don't care who you're saving it for. Fix up my boy Rodney with those seats."

"Yes, Mr. Johnson."

"I'm here with my aunt," I told him.

"Well, the whole executive box is yours." Some people had spotted him and were beginning to crowd around us. "I had better bid you farewell before I'm late for my first scene."

"Good luck," I shouted.

"In this biz we say, 'Break a leg.'"

"Okay, then break a leg!"

I walked off with the usher. When we got to my aunt, I leaned over and whispered, "Ready to see where we are?" At first Sir Snottingham wouldn't get up and just stared straight ahead, but when he saw my aunt take my hand, he followed us pretty quickly—all the way to a private box where everything was covered in red velvet overlooking the stage.

"My, these seats are absolutely spectacular. Aren't they, Edward?" my aunt asked.

After a long pause, I heard what sounded like a dog snarling and noticed Snottingham pulling on his mustache.

My aunt continued. "I said, 'I think these are the finest seats in the house.' Don't you agree, Edward?"

"Yeah, Ed," I chimed in, "influential people like me know how to get things done. Wouldn't you agree? Look, we can even see backstage." By now he was furiously twisting both ends of his mustache at once. "Do you see Victor Johnson waving to us?" I wasn't lying. He was off to the side giving us a thumbs-up. When he spotted my aunt, he made a slight bow before blowing her a kiss.

My aunt laughed and exclaimed, "Rodney, you're amazing. Isn't he amazing, Edward?" It was the final straw.

"AAAArrrghhhhhh!" he howled. I looked over at him. He had actually pulled off his mustache! He stumbled back through the opening behind the executive box and ran off, holding his mouth.

My aunt laughed. "Oh, that Sir Edward, he's always up to something."

For the next two hours we watched the show, and as the curtain dropped, my aunt turned to me. "Rodney, that was the best play I have ever seen and these are the best seats I've ever had in all the world. You are simply full of surprises and full of adventure. You'll have to go to London with me next year. Oh, and I think we'll keep it a secret from Sir Edward Snottingham. What do you say?"

"Sounds like a plan, Aunt Evelyn," I answered, smiling, as Victor Johnson walked onstage to thunderous applause. Like his performance, my visit to New York had been a rousing success.

Chapter 23

A PECULIAR SENSE OF DREAD

I was exhausted Monday morning, and my feet still hurt from pounding the Manhattan pavement, but I felt great. I was back in Garrettsville, where I was popular at school, where Jessica seemed to like me as much as I liked her, and where I had made so many friends. Best of all, summer was only a month away. As I rode to school that morning, I looked out the window thinking that things had never been better. Little did I guess that someone even more frightening than Josh or Toby or Rocco was about to turn my life upside down for the rest of the school year.

Walking in the hallway before class, I was busy telling the fellas of my adventures in New York when Rishi interrupted.

"I still haven't told you the big news. . . ."

"Rishi, close your mouth!" It was Mrs. Lutzkraut shouting at us. "And, Rodney," she continued, "I don't think there's anything special about playing hooky from school so you can run around a city." Evidently she had been spying on our conversation. As we stood in the crowded hallway, she glanced up and waved her hand. "Mr. Feebletop, can I have a word, please?"

"Yes, Mrs. Lutzkraut. What can I do for you?"

"Rodney," she snapped. "Come over here." I walked past the line of students in the hall and stood before the two of them. Mrs. Lutzkraut's eyes twinkled slightly before she began. "Mr. Feebletop, it has just come to my attention that Mr. Rathbone here was absent Friday to go on vacation. I thought you ought to know about it, since you've been trying to enforce a strict attendance policy."

Mr. Feebletop sighed and looked like he was upset that he had to deal with this. "Mrs. Lutzkraut is right, Rodney. Attendance is an issue."

Mrs. Lutzkraut interrupted, "What do you intend to do, Mr. Feebletop?"

He looked down at me and shook his head. "You know, Rodney, we just got over the basketball incident with Mrs. Whiner."

Again Lutzkraut interrupted. "Mr. Feebletop, on the phone his mother distinctly said he had laryngitis. She lied to me. . . ."

"I wish *you* had laryngitis!" my mouth exploded. It just came out. I didn't like anyone calling my mom a liar.

"Unacceptable, Rodney!" Mr. Feebletop yelled. It was the first time I had seen him mad like that and I knew I was in for it. "Go to my office right now." He turned and stormed off toward the lobby.

Mrs. Lutzkraut gave me a sickening smirk as she led the class toward room 217.

"That was dumb, Rodney," Jessica whispered as she walked by. "Now you'll probably miss all the fun end-of-year events coming up."

"Jessica!" Mrs. Lutzkraut hollered. Jessica didn't look up to reply. She just tucked her head down and high-tailed it, leaving me alone.

Mr. Feebletop was swiveling in his chair, looking back at his picture of Tom Seaver. When I came in, he turned around and had a stern look on his face. "Rodney, you should know better. You must be respectful to adults. You crossed the line and did it right in front of me."

"I'm sorry, Mr. Feebletop. Sometimes my mouth kind of acts on its own."

"Yes, well, a big mouth gets you into trouble, and before we discuss what you said, we should talk about your little vacation. There's plenty of time in the summer to go away. It's not acceptable to just pick up, pretend you're sick, and shoot off. . . ."

"I know," I explained, "but I had a chance to visit my great-aunt in New York. She bought tickets for me and some friends to see the Mets at Citi Field."

Suddenly he was on his feet, practically leaning over the desk. "You saw the Mets?"

"Yep. It was awesome. And I kind of got you a souvenir."

"Souvenir?" He tried to keep a straight face but I noticed a faint smile begin to appear.

"I got you this."

I reached into my jacket pocket and flipped him the baseball. He caught it, examined it, and fell back in his seat with a gasp. His hands began shaking. Then I noticed his eyes start to tear up. He opened his mouth to speak but could form no words. Finally, after hyperventilating for a bit, he cleared his throat and read, "'To my greatest fan, Mr. Feebletop. All the best! Tom Seaver'."

"I knew you would like it," I told him, "but I'm sorry I had to give it to you today, I mean, after getting you mad and everything. I really am sorry for mouthing off like that in the hallway."

"Well, Rodney, I know these things happen," he said, regaining a bit of his composure, "and I know you feel bad. Let me think about a punishment. Right now, though, I have to address the school regarding field day. I think you'll like what you hear. Despite today's, um, unfortunate incident, I made a decision last week that involves you, and I am going to stick to it. Now hurry back to homeroom. And Rodney . . ."

"Yes, Mr. Feebletop?"

"Was Tom Seaver nice? Did you tell him about me? Did he mention Eddie Kranepool . . ."

"Mr. Feebletop," a secretary called from the door, "the announcements."

"Oh, quite so. Now, where was I?"

I walked into class and sat down at my desk. Seeing me, Mrs. Lutzkraut flashed a twisted grin. "Rodney, I've just finished telling the class that next Friday is field day, and that participation is a privilege. Not everybody needs to participate." She wasn't finished. Armed with the knowledge that she'd finally gotten me, and thoroughly enjoying the moment, she twirled a sharp pencil around between her fingers. "I think on field day, while you're sitting in the principal's office, it would be a good time for you to write an essay about responsibility." She was sure Mr. Feebletop had suspended me from participating. The next thing I heard was his voice on the loudspeaker.

"Good morning, Baber! What a glorious morning!" Mrs. Lutzkraut stared at the speaker with a smile as he continued. "I wanted to make a few announcements before the morning pledge. As most of you already know, next Friday is field day. The school will be divided by class into two teams, white and blue. The following classes are on the white team. . . ." He rattled off a list. We were on the blue team. Then he continued. "This year we have a special treat for one class of the winning team. This year it's Ms. Dearing's class for the white and Mrs. Lutzkraut's for the blue.

The winner of field day will be going to . . . Super Adventure amusement park!" The class erupted into a cheer. I wasn't really sure what Super Adventure was, but I noticed Jessica was clapping and Rishi was practically jumping to the ceiling.

"Rodney! That's the big news I've been trying to tell you. My mom's on the PTA field day committee, and . . ."

"Rishi," Mrs. Lutzkraut cut in, "I'm sorry to break this to you, but the way Mr. Feebletop punishes unruly students late in the year is by making them sit in his office for field day. It's a shame, but I imagine that this is what Rodney just learned for himself." The fake sorrow in her voice was nauseating. "And if he can't participate, then he can't be on the winning team, which means no Super Adventure for him."

Rishi slumped down in his chair and Jessica's eyes looked wet. Toby, however, looked like he'd just won the Lotto jackpot.

"One more thing," Mr. Feebletop's voice crackled above us. "I forgot to announce this year's honorary field day captains. For the blue team, the one leading the squad, I have selected Baber's newest star pupil, Rodney Rathbone! Way to go, Rodney! The white captain . . ."

I couldn't hear Mr. Feebletop continue because my class was cheering and jumping up and down. Mrs. Lutzkraut's face turned as red as an apple and the pencil in her hand snapped in half. As if in a trance, she turned and gazed out the window, one side of her face twitching up and down.

She was muttering to herself now, almost like she was talking to someone on the other side of the windowpane. Rishi twirled his finger by the side of his head.

What happened next was just as strange. All at once, Mrs. Lutzkraut relaxed. She became calm and serene, but as she turned back to class I saw a bizarre gleam in her eye, one I'd never witnessed before.

"Children, take out your math books, open them to page 372. . . ." Her voice was softer than usual, a welcome break to the rest of the class . . . but I wasn't so sure.

For most of the morning she remained quiet, sitting at her desk wiping a tiny spot over and over again. Finally the clock hit twelve thirty. Lunchtime. We lined up as usual, but instead of leading us down the corridor, Mrs. Lutzkraut called across the hall. "Ms. Dearing, would you mind walking my class down to the cafeteria with yours? I need a few moments to congratulate my class's new field day captain."

"No problem," Ms. Dearing replied sweetly. "Well done, Rodney. You must be very proud of him, Mrs. Lutzkraut."

"Oh . . . *proud* isn't the word for it!" she answered, smiling widely. Ms. Dearing nodded and led the classes away. For a moment we watched the lines disappear around the bend in the hall.

"Let's step inside, shall we?" I walked back in, feeling a peculiar sense of dread, worse than all the other senses of dread I'd experienced so often in my life. "Close the door, will you, Rodney?" I gulped but did what she asked.

She had returned to her desk, and while she still smiled, it did nothing to calm my anxiety. She reminded me of a vampire, happy that she had a young, sweet victim all to herself. "Come closer, I won't bite." My heart pounded in my chest. "I just wanted to congratulate you. I realize that Mr. Feebletop, in his infinite wisdom, has bestowed a notable honor on you. Not such a big deal to you, though, right? You seem capable of so many wonderful things, like wrapping our esteemed principal around your little finger." Her voice, dripping with sarcasm, flowed out through a perfectly gleeful and evil veil. "I hope you're enjoying it. I hope you have enjoyed it all, because as of now, everything good in your life ends."

I eyed the door. "Oh no," she continued. "Running won't save you. Rodney, you are what is known as a bad seed. Most of the fools around here don't see it, but I do. And do you know what I do when I find a bad seed?" She moved a step closer.

I opened my mouth, but was too scared to say anything.

"What? No smart-aleck remark? I'm disappointed in you." She was twirling something silver in her hand that looked like scissors. "I'm going to enjoy this," she muttered. I got ready to jump out the window. "I'm going to enjoy this last month of school," she continued.

"I will be savoring each and every day." The scissors flashed in the light and I realized it was just a silver pen, but my fear rose anyway as she took yet another step closer. Finally she leaned right over me. "Now get out! Go have a nice lunch, *captain*."

Chapter 24

FIELD DAY

I was quiet all day, my head swimming with nightmarish images. It wasn't until well after school that my heart rate slowed to below a million and my brain could clearly pay attention to the outside world.

"I can't believe Feebletop made you captain after what you said to Lutzkraut," Rishi was saying as we walked through the neighborhood with a bunch of friends. "I keep flashing back to that look on her face . . . priceless. The best part, though, is that with you as captain, we can't lose."

Huh? I didn't like the sound of that.

"We have to win!" Slim added.

"Why?" Greg asked.

"Super Adventure!" Slim yelled in his face.

"I'm not worried, though," Rishi continued. "We can't lose. Dave is like lightning fast, and Rodney, well, he's Rodney Rathbone. It's going to be awesome at

Super Adventure. Besides the regular coaster, they built a new one, Destination Death."

I didn't want to hear any more. First of all, I hate roller coasters, but it wasn't just that. Half the school was expecting me to lead them to victory. Meanwhile, every time I've held a key position during an athletic event, I've choked and lost it for my team. Just last year back in New York, I tripped right before the finish line on the hundred-yard dash. Thank God Dave was running it at Baber's field day and not me. The hundred-yard dash was worth the most points.

"Chicken Legs McGraw is on the white team, and he's real fast," Greg was pointing out.

Rishi smiled. "True, but next to Dave, he looks like a slug."

We continued walking toward the old abandoned school near the McThuggs. I realized that the pressure was squarely on Dave and not me. I began to relax a little—until the hairs on the back of my neck suddenly rose! Something felt eerily wrong. I glanced behind us. A red car was inching along, keeping pace. I looked at the driver. She wore a scarf and had big sunglasses. Something about her nose looked familiar, but I couldn't be sure. Then the car drove below a tree and the bright glare on the windshield disappeared, revealing another woman sitting in the passenger seat. It was Mrs. Lutzkraut, following us. Following me! Just as I was about to yell, the car sped off.

"What's with that guy?" Rishi asked, pointing at the car.

"That was no guy. It was Mrs. Lutzkraut and I think Long Nose might have been with her!"

"Ha-ha! Nice one, Rodney," Rishi laughed, slapping my back.

"No, I'm serious, she was . . ."

"Always kidding, this guy."

I didn't say any more. They wouldn't have believed me. Heck, I'm not sure I believed it. Was it her? I felt jittery all over, made an excuse to leave, and went straight home.

Almost before I knew it, field day arrived. I got dressed that morning and pulled on a blue T-shirt. Besides a few odd, knowing looks, Mrs. Lutzkraut hadn't done anything else, and I approached the day with only the mild dread of having to lead half the school to victory.

My mom wished me good luck as I headed toward the door. Penny wasn't quite as generous.

"I hope you don't mess up like in New York," she teased.

"Penny!" my mother scolded. "Wish your brother luck."

"Okay, good luck trying not to mess up."

With those words of encouragement, I said good-bye and walked to the bus stop. I heard the deep noise of the bus engine before I saw the familiar yellowish gold. As it approached it seemed louder than usual, and when I climbed aboard I realized that the racket wasn't from the engine alone—the students were cheering. Every kid in blue was chanting, "Rod! Rod! Rod!" Kids on the white team eyed me nervously, but said nothing. With each cheer, a knot in my stomach twisted.

We walked from the bus into the cafeteria, where Mrs. Lutzkraut, dressed in green, picked us up. I noticed Ms. Dearing was in a white tank top. "No blue, Mrs. Lutzkraut?" Rishi asked.

Her scowl, ever quick to show through her wrinkles, grew deeper as she blared, "Keep that mouth shut if you know what's good for you. Teachers should be impartial. I root for all students to do their best, and it doesn't matter which class they're from." Then she noticed me standing nearby. "And besides, Rishi, I would worry more about your captain letting you down than the color of my clothing."

How did she know about my secret fear? It was almost like she was a witch who could read my mind. This was supposed to be Baber Intermediate, not Hogwarts! I was happy when we finally lined up and headed out to the field.

Kayla, her arms folded across her chest, came up to me and demanded, "Okay, Captain, get to work." Did she think I'd be taking on half the school by myself? Most of the events were individual races, and a captain didn't really do much more than anyone else. I would have pointed this out to her, but people started chanting Rod again.

For a while it looked like my nervousness was unfounded. With the exception of the obstacle course, where Slim got stuck in a tire, we won every morning event, and it was during the class vs. class battle of Capture the Flag that Rishi ran by saying, "We have it won! All we have to do now is watch Dave win the hundred-yard dash this afternoon. We can lose the tug-of-war later and still win." I nodded coolly, but I exhaled one giant sigh of relief. The rush of air got caught in my throat, however, as a scene unfolded before my eyes.

Dave did a spin move during Capture the Flag and ran by a white team tagger, but he hadn't noticed Josh slicing toward him from his blind side. Josh clearly didn't care about the score in the game. He was going in with a lowered shoulder. Dave saw him, but it was too late. He and Josh collided with a sickening smack. Dave crunched to the ground in a heap and didn't get up.

Our team stood in shock, watching Dave on the ground holding his ankle. "I can almost hear the roller coasters already," Josh murmured, walking off the field to the water table.

I didn't say anything. One of my friends was on the ground crying. We huddled around him, and soon a kind, soothing tongue arrived.

"Stop that blubbering, Rishi," Mrs. Lutzkraut snapped. "What did you hurt? Why are you crying?"

Jessica turned to her. "Dave's actually the one hurt, Mrs. Lutzkraut."

Dave, who was clearly in pain, sat with gritted teeth consoling Rishi, who was stretched on the ground shouting, "Why? Why? Why?"

"Zip it, Rishi," Mrs. Lutzkraut barked, "or I'll give you a reason to cry." Then she stared down at Dave. "You'll have to go to the nurse. It seems your field day will end early." For a moment she looked slightly compassionate. Seeing me changed that. "Don't stand there gawking. Line up to go inside. We have lunch, but before that, we need to go over your homework assignments from Tuesday."

Our class was somber walking in. We sat down and Mrs. Lutzkraut handed out essays we had written. After returning every paper but mine, she stood over my desk and whispered, "Tsk tsk," under her breath. What did that mean? She walked to the head of the class. I raised my hand.

"Yes, Rodney?"

"Um, you didn't give me back my paper."

"That's because you never handed one in. I have given you an incomplete on the assignment." Her eyes were gleaming and looking straight into mine.

"But Mrs. Lutzkraut, I *did* hand it in."

Her right eye began to twitch. "Are you calling me a liar?"

"Well no, but I definitely wrote the assignment, and

I'm *pretty sure* I turned it in." Suddenly she had me doubting myself.

"Well I'm *pretty sure* you're going to fail if I give you another incomplete." I heard some kids chuckle, and I didn't like it one bit.

"That was dumb, not handing in your paper," Jessica mentioned as we returned outside for recess.

"I did! Mrs. Lutzkraut must have lost it . . . maybe on purpose."

"Oh come on, Rodney, she'd never do that."

"She did, though. Ever since Feebletop made me captain, she's been out to get me. She really . . ." I was cut off by Kayla and our friends, who were gathering around.

"What are we going to do now, Captain?" Kayla asked.

"Yeah, what's the plan?" Samantha joined in. "Chicken Legs McGraw will win it for them now and we'll never get to go to Super Adventure. Is there anyone in our class who can beat him?"

"There is," Rishi calmly answered. *Oh good,* I thought, until I heard him continue, "Rodney's the captain. He'll have to beat him."

They all looked relieved, but I instantly remembered my past running events. Something always seemed to go wrong. I couldn't be counted on to win.

"Rodney?" Greg asked. "You all right?"

"Of course he is," Rishi answered.

"I have a plan," I announced. It had hit me just as Greg snapped me out of my trip down misery lane.

"You see, he has a . . . wait," Rishi asked. "We already know you're going to win the hundred-yard dash for us. Why do we need a plan?"

"You said it'd be close," I explained. "Well I have a way to win the tug-of-war for sure, and I've done the math. We just have to win one of the last two events to win field day."

"That's my captain," Jessica said.

"Rodney, I have never doubted you," Rishi explained, "but there's no way we can beat Dearing's class in the tug-of-war. They're twice our size, especially with Josh pulling anchorman."

"Shhhh, keep it down. Toby is right over there. Unless you want Josh to know my plan, don't let him hear what we're saying. Everyone, come over here. All right . . ." They crowded in. "Well, you know what happens if we let go of the rope at the same time?" I asked.

"Yeah," Kayla said. "They'll go flying, but the rope will go with them and they'll win."

"No, Kayla, they won't win. I've been looking at how far the rope must travel for it to cross the line for a victory. If they all fall they'll pull it, but it won't go beyond the line. We just pick it up and yank it back. They'll be so shocked, most of them will let go, and those who don't will go for a little ride."

After a few more explanations, my blue team knew

what to do. As the field day competitions resumed, the kids in white were laughing and smiling. With Dave out of the way, they were sure they were heading to Super Adventure. Armed with my plan, I wasn't sweating it.

We lifted the thick brown rope. I was third from the front behind Rishi and an unsuspecting Toby. Jessica was right behind me and Slim was in the back with Greg. Ms. Dearing's class dropped their smiles and looked at us with grim, determined faces. I could see Josh way at the end, anchorman. He looked ready to pull us over all by himself. I also noticed that Mrs. Lutzkraut had come over to watch the big event.

"When I blow the whistle, begin pulling, but not until then," Mr. Ball, the gym teacher, announced. Many of us were already yanking a bit. The rope was taut. I felt alive and ready.

The whistle blared and the rope lurched forward. I could feel it slide a bit in my hands and my feet began to give way. I wanted to wait a couple of seconds, but we were being pulled hard and I didn't think we could last.

"Now!" I shouted. Everyone in our class, except Toby, let go of the rope. The result was immediate and impressive. Toby, still holding on, went flying through the air. The white shirts went down fast and hard. I heard a loud *"Ooooffffff!"* from many of them and, true to my prediction, the rope hadn't gone far enough.

"Now!" I shouted again. We all grabbed the rope and yanked. Most of Ms. Dearing's class had let go and it was easy as pie to pull it back over our line. We all cheered. We had won field day and were so busy dancing around yelling that it took a few minutes to hear Mrs. Lutzkraut shrieking above the commotion. Gradually we stopped cheering and stood silent, looking at her.

"Letting go of the rope is not allowed in the tug-of-war," she was shouting, making sure Mr. Ball—and two other students in particular—could hear. "It's dangerous. Rodney, I distinctly heard you yell 'Now' right before the rope went flying. This was all your idea, and now look what you did. I hope Josh and Toby weren't hurt by your actions!"

At this I looked over at the white team. They were a sad sight, a large pile of bodies, with one boy buried at the bottom. With their own force, they must have fallen backward onto Josh. I could see his face, full of pain, rage, and embarrassment. His eyeballs were flaming red and staring my way. Then I saw another unwelcome sight. Toby had flown a good ten feet and landed in the one puddle left over from last week's rain. He, too, was glaring directly at me through a brown, smeared face.

"Was this some kind of joke on me and Josh?" he yelled.

My dumb plan had reawakened the beasts. Josh was pushing people off him looking ready to kill someone. Toby was walking over to him. Gripped by a surging sense of panic, I almost didn't hear Mr. Ball add, "Thank you, Mrs. Lutzkraut, for being such an objective witness.

But I'm afraid this means your class is disqualified in the tug-of-war."

The white team cheered. Rishi threw himself to the ground in dismay. Most of my classmates couldn't believe that their own teacher had ruined it for them, but they also gave me dirty looks, blaming me for the loss. Mrs. Lutzkraut stared in my direction and suddenly stuck out her tongue. "Look!" I screamed, but it was too late. She had turned around.

Kayla muttered, "Nice going, Captain." A group of downcast blue shirts wandered off, clearly giving me the cold shoulder.

Slim said, "Don't feel bad. Once you win the hundred-yard dash, they'll forgive you."

I wandered over to the starting line, no longer worrying about losing the tug-of-war or failing as captain or even Mrs. Lutzkraut. What had seemed so important just moments ago was nothing now. I had bigger problems. Toby was talking to Josh and pointing at me. Josh turned my way. All he needed was horns and he would have looked like a bull ready to charge.

And that's just what he did. With a savage yell, Josh flung Toby to the side and began running straight at me. I looked around. There was only one person close to me. It was Mrs. Lutzkraut, and believe it or not, I was relieved to see her. "Mrs. Lutzkraut, look! Josh is running this way. He's going to kill me! Mrs. Lutzkraut?"

If she heard me, she didn't respond. I looked up at

her in shock just as Mr. Ball fired the pistol to start the race. Instead of waiting around for Josh to trample me, I took off running. I ran like my life depended on it, which it probably did. I ran faster than I ever had before. My panicked, maniacal, fear-driven run was so fast that I escaped Josh and dusted all the competition, including Chicken Legs McGraw.

At the other side of the hundred yards, I was still running on instinct, like a rabbit escaping a fox, and I didn't really understand why I was met by a white ribbon hitting me in the chest, and why Mr. Feebletop was raising my hand into the air, and why Mr. Ball was yelling, "Blue wins!" and why Mrs. Lutzkraut was pulling out clumps of hair, and why every blue-clad student was encircling me and cheering. I had won field day without even knowing it.

Chapter 25

I OVERHEAR A PLOT

As the crowd swarmed around me, Rishi came running up and shook me by the shoulders. "You did it, Rodney! I knew you would!" Mr. Feebletop was clapping. Jessica was smiling. The noise was deafening. I was being turned, grabbed, and patted. Lost in the crazed excitement, I spun around with a dumb smile on my face.

"Oh boy," I mumbled, smile fading. I had turned right into Josh.

Then he smiled. An actual big grin. Wow, could this really be? It seemed that even *he* was excited about my great run. Before I knew it he stuck out his hand to shake mine. This was super. I reached out and shook it—and a bear trap snapped shut on my fingers. I looked down and saw it was actually Josh's hand . . . crushing mine.

He pulled me in close. "I'll get you alone sooner or later," he whispered, "and when I do . . . you're dead."

He leaned back, clicked his smile back on, and letting go of my poor, throbbing hand disappeared into the crowd. I didn't know how much longer I could keep up the fake Superman thing, but I really didn't have a choice at this point.

"That was nice of him to congratulate you," Greg said from behind me.

"Yeah, real nice," I choked, walking off.

Before I got too far Jessica met me. "That was the most incredible run I've ever seen. I really can't believe some of the things you do." She smiled at me.

That makes two of us, I thought.

"You know," she added more shyly, "next Friday is the big end-of-year dance."

I decided to make use of my hero status while it lasted. "Jessica, I know I'll see you there, but can I take you to the dance, like officially?"

"Officially?" she smiled. "Do you mean like a date?"

Luckily my face was still red from the hundred-yard dash. She couldn't see me blush as I answered, "Yes, a date."

"Okay. You can pick me up around seven. Rodney, are you listening?"

Mrs. Lutzkraut was staring at me and shaking her fist in the air. Suddenly Mr. Feebletop called out to her. "Ah, the raised fist of triumph!" She jumped like a little kid caught doing something wrong. I turned back in time to see Kayla dragging Jessica off somewhere, but it didn't matter. I had asked Jessica to the dance and she had actually said yes.

I was consumed by mixed emotions. Things were awesome with Jessica, and my usual group of friends loved me all the more. On the other hand, my worst enemies were more fired up than ever. There were two weeks left till the end of the year, and they'd be dangerous weeks. I'd have to be extra-careful and keep my eyes wide open.

I took my first precautions on Monday morning, standing in front of the class. Making sure I had plenty of witnesses, I announced, "I am now handing in my book report. It is on *Stormbreaker*, by Anthony Horowitz." I laid it down on Mrs. Lutzkraut's desk.

"Do you think you could hand in your assignment without comment?" Despite her little zinger, I couldn't risk any more missing assignments and walked straight back to my desk. I noticed her eyeing the report in a strange way. Then she looked up at me, smiled, and stated, "This is going to be a glorious week. Can't you just feel it?" I felt something, all right. Shivers down my spine! My mind raced, trying to figure out what she had in store for me.

Concern about Mrs. Lutzkraut's next move swept through my brain the rest of the morning. Even later when we walked down to lunch I kept my eye on her, ready for anything. Arriving at the cafeteria, I sat down with the boys and got ready to eat, until I realized I had forgotten my lunch. It was in the last place I wanted to return alone.

"Where's your lunch?" Slim asked. He usually finished anything left by the rest of us and was probably wondering about my dessert.

"I forgot it in the classroom."

"Well, go get it!"

"I'm not really hungry," I lied, my stomach growling.

"Hey, Mrs. Canasta! Can Rodney get his lunch from class?" Slim called to the aide who had replaced Long Nose. She was very nice and rushed over.

"Absolutely. Rodney, go get it." I didn't want to go. Long Nose would have told me no. For once I missed her nastiness.

"Go on, go on," Slim prodded.

Reluctantly, I walked out and continued down the hall. Maybe Mrs. Lutzkraut wouldn't be there. I walked extra-quietly and when I got to the room, I peered in through the open door. The classroom was empty. Quickly, I darted to the closet, rifled through my backpack, and grabbed the lunch.

"This has been an excellent little talk, Joshua," a voice sounded by the classroom door. Frightened, I moved farther into the closet. "You understand what to do?"

"Yeah," Josh answered.

"Excellent. Now get back to the cafeteria."

Josh walked away, but Mrs. Lutzkraut walked in and sat down behind her desk. I shuddered to think what the two of them had been talking about. It also occurred to me I was stuck in the closet. Maybe if I just hid for a minute she'd . . .

"Who's back there? I can see your arm!" Her voice boomed out across the classroom. I had no choice but to stick my head out. She stood up from her desk, and I noticed that weird twitch return to her face. "I should have known it was you. How much did you hear?"

"Hear? I, uh, just got, uh . . ."

"Being that you are a perpetual liar, one would imagine you would be better at it." She was now walking toward me. Instinctively, I inched toward the door. "It's really no matter, though. It will be an evening to remember, don't you agree?"

What was she talking about? She definitely thought I had heard more than I did. "Uh, yeah, an evening to remember," I repeated, still inching away.

"Well?" she asked.

"Umm, well what?"

"*Ummm*, aren't you going to go eat your lunch?"

"Yes, right away." And with that I bolted out of class, more confused and worried than ever.

That afternoon I tried desperately to figure out what she had in store for me. My friends were no help whatsoever. When I tried to explain that Mrs. Lutzkraut was plotting something evil, they laughed and told me I read too many scary books. I didn't say anything, but the truth is that I don't ever read scary books. I have enough fears in the real world to keep me busy. Like having a crazy lady plotting against me. Or was she? Maybe this whole thing with Mrs. Lutzkraut was in my mind.

Wanting to be alone to sort things out, I left my carefree, happy friends at the bus stop and took the "long cut" back home. After a few blocks I felt the now-familiar presence of a car creeping along a few paces behind me. My mouth ran dry and I couldn't breathe. Maybe I was imagining it. I gave a quick glance over my shoulder—and saw a red car. Not daring to wait and see who or what was driving, I took off. The car picked up speed behind me. This was it. I was alone this time—and running for my life.

I cut left across a front yard and around the side of a house. I didn't slow down in the backyard but just kept running right past a lady gardening who barely managed a hey! before I flipped myself over her chain-link fence. I took off across the green grass of someone else's backyard and slipped on a pile of dog doo, but didn't even have time to say yuck. I blitzed out into the front yard and angled out into the road, where I stood panting, looking all around me.

Down the block, at the cross street, I thought I saw the hood of the red car sticking out slightly from behind a hedge. I was still catching my breath when the car suddenly lurched forward and turned in my direction.

It was enough to get me moving again. As I ran through some woods that eventually led to the back of my house, I realized that everything had gone too far. Someone was going to get hurt—and that someone was me. My friends didn't believe it when I told them what Mrs. Lutzkraut was doing. They assumed I was making up a story and being silly, but this couldn't continue. I had to tell my parents. At least they would believe me.

Close to my house, I sat down on an old stump to catch my breath. Knowing I was about to get help from my mom and dad, I felt the first sense of relief in weeks. After a minute or two I got up and finished the walk through the woods. I was almost smiling as I strode in through the back door. "Hey Mom! Where are you? I need to talk to you!"

"I'm right in here, honey. Come see who just popped over." Was it Rishi? Aunt Evelyn? I rushed in.

"Hello, Rodney," said a familiar voice. My blood ran cold. Sitting there in my father's chair was Mrs. Lutzkraut.

Chapter 26

THE BIG DANCE

"Can you believe who's paying us a visit?" My mom smiled, holding a pair of teacups in her hands. A scream tried to escape my mouth but I locked my lips together. After gingerly exhaling a deep breath, I attempted a response.

"Ahh." I couldn't say any more.

"Sit down, Rodney. Mrs. Lutzkraut was just talking to me about the school year. Don't look so panicked. We're discussing good things. Mrs. Lutzkraut, you were saying . . ."

"Yes, Mrs. Rathbone. You know I think the world of your son, and I am so thankful that he moved here this year and joined my class." My mom beamed. I almost puked. "Parents need to hear good news, too, you know. And that really is why I'm here. You need to know just how impressed I've been with your son."

"Rodney, isn't that nice of Mrs. Lutzkraut? Could you imagine having a nicer teacher?"

"Ahh."

"It's okay, Mrs. Rathbone. I don't like to put students on the spot. Oh, one more thing. You may know there's a dance this Friday night."

My head was spinning, but when she mentioned the dance my intestines twisted. That's what she had meant when I'd overheard her say, "an evening to remember . . ." It was the one thing I had been looking forward to most and now my big night with Jessica would be ruined.

My mom said, "Yes, I read about the dance in the PTA bulletin."

"Well, I know how shy Rodney can be . . ."

What???

". . . and boys his age will make any excuse to get out of a dance, but I really believe going to this dance will do wonders for his socialization." Then she turned and addressed me directly. "Rodney, we will *all* be so disappointed if you choose not to attend."

"Mrs. Lutzkraut," my mom began, "I just want to thank you for this year. Rodney has done a great job adjusting to his new town and school, and I can see it's because of you and your hard work."

Was this all really happening?

"No other teacher I know would take time from her busy schedule to make a personal stop and discuss a student's well-being."

My well-being? The lady was busy planning my execution.

"It's my pleasure," Mrs. Lutzkraut replied, setting down the teacup and rising to shake my mom's hand. "You never described how lovely your home was, Rodney. Oh, and don't forget the dance Friday night. *We'll be waiting for you.*" She turned her head so my mom couldn't see and gave me a little wink.

We walked to the door. All of a sudden the red car pulled up. "Here's my ride now," Mrs. Lutzkraut announced. "My friend and I so enjoy driving on these late spring days. I'll see you tomorrow, Rodney." The door closed and I watched her walk down the steps.

"Oh Rodney, you are truly blessed to have such a wonderful teacher," my mom said, walking into the kitchen.

"Mom, the woman's crazy! She . . ."

"Rodney, Mrs. Lutzkraut is one of those special teachers. She may be demanding, but she's the type that can change a student's life forever. Now go wash up for dinner." Well, she was right about that. I had no doubt she'd be changing my life. I just hoped I'd be around to see how it turned out.

I wish I could tell you more about the days leading up to the dance, but all week I was fixated on the doom surrounding Friday night. Jessica got more excited as it got closer, and I fought to act the same, only my dream-come-true had become a nightmare. By the time Friday rolled around, any excitement I felt about Jessica was squashed by the occasional evil grins from Josh and Toby and Mrs. Lutzkraut. The three were in cahoots, and tonight was the night.

That afternoon, I found myself at home, looking in the mirror and thinking over my problems. My brown eyes staring back at me were red and frightened. I was angry with myself. *Why are you such a chicken?* I asked my reflection.

Duh, my reflection seemed to answer, *Josh is going to kill you tonight. Stay home and do something else. Read a book. You can even have a tea party with your sister and her dolls. Just don't go to that dance.*

My reflection seemed to make sense, and my sister would sure love it. But then I got mad at the guy in the mirror. Didn't he realize Jessica was going to be at the dance and just waiting to . . . ?

You can't kiss a girl if you're dead, my reflection answered. He had a point. But then again, if I didn't go tonight I'd have to face Josh eventually anyway, and what could Mrs. Lutzkraut really do? There'd be lots of other adults around. Besides, the best-looking, coolest girl in the grade was waiting to be my date. Maybe I was tougher than I gave myself credit for. I took a long hard look at my reflection, exhaled, and finally, after weighing all the options, turned my back on the mirror. I strolled confidently out of the bathroom and down the hall to the top of the steps. "Penny!" I yelled. "Count me in for tea. Just don't sit me next to Mrs. Puffdoodle!"

"Yay!" Penny cheered from the den.

My mom, however, stepped out of her room and gave me a funny look. "Rodney, what are you doing? You need to be getting ready for the dance tonight."

"Mom, I don't think I'm going. I'm not feeling that great."

She smiled and took me by the shoulder. "I think I know what this is about."

"You do?" I asked, shocked.

"Yes, honey, I know you're worried about dancing. Mrs. Lutzkraut warned me you would probably be embarrassed to dance. Well, it's nothing to worry about. You'll do great. Now come into the bathroom and let me fix your hair. Your father will drop you and Jessica off and then come back at the end to drive everyone home."

"But Mom, I don't think I want to . . ."

"But Mom nothing. I have the perfect shirt for you. These jeans will look the best. Hmm, no, maybe these khakis, no, the jeans. Okay, shoes. You can't wear sneakers. Here, put on your black dress shoes. . . ."

I looked down at the shoes she was referring to. They were black, dressy, and supershiny. I could see my face reflected in the gleaming surface. I looked disgusted. "Mom, I'm not wearing those. You bought them for Mrs. Geller's son's wedding."

"So, they're perfect. . . ."

"No, they're too hard and slippery, and I'll be the

only one wearing shoes like those. I'll look like a fool," I whined.

"Nonsense, now let's see about . . ."

I tried to argue, but when my mom is focused on a task, there's no stopping her. She had me dressed, pressed, wiped, and tucked before I could blink. As my dad and I pulled out of the driveway, I looked back and saw my mom waving happily. My sister, walking with her teapot, wasn't smiling.

The dance was in the Baber gym. The parents had decorated it with streamers and balloons. A DJ had set up a booth at the far end. As Jessica and I entered, the DJ's big speakers were already blaring the most recent hit song. Jessica joined the girls dancing down in front as I quickly looked around. No sign of Josh or Toby. Maybe they weren't coming. That made sense. A dance didn't really seem like their kind of thing. A huge weight lifted off my shoulders. Even though Mrs. Lutzkraut was there, talking to Mr. Feebletop and Ms. Dearing, she didn't seem very interested in me. I decided to join my friends.

Dave was still on crutches. Perfect prey. Sure enough, Kayla walked by and asked, "Wanna dance, Dave?" She giggled, then dragged my hopping friend into the middle of the girls, who all thought a boy on crutches was great and danced around him.

"Nice shoes." Slim laughed, looking down at my feet.

Rishi added an, "Oh man, check those things out."

I didn't respond. My mind had drifted elsewhere. It wasn't Josh or Toby or Mrs. Lutzkraut that had grabbed my attention. It was a girl who looked better than ever. Her blond hair glided in the air as she walked my way. When she came up to me and grabbed my hand, I thought I might die. "You ready to dance?" Jessica asked.

I nodded, feeling good all over. Looking back at my two gawking friends, I winked. "Must be the shoes."

We strolled into the crowd and began dancing. I felt a little silly at first, especially with the lights reflecting off my goofy shoes, but after a few minutes Jessica was the only one on my mind. She had on a blue dress that matched her eyes, and once or twice her hair blew past my face. I could feel it graze my cheek and I could smell her shampoo.

We looked at each other through the flashing colored lights and laughing crowd. She came closer and said, "Let's get some soda."

We passed through the doors and walked up to a table in the lobby loaded down with cups, soda bottles, and chips. Rishi and Slim were there eating out of the Dorito bowl. Ignoring them, I filled our cups. One fizzed up and Jessica leaned down and drank off the foam. I watched her in a trance and didn't notice the change in the room. After a few moments, I saw that Rishi and Slim had stopped eating and were staring behind me. Despite having a brown soda mustache, there was nothing funny about Jessica's frightened expression.

How could I have been so stupid? How could I have let my guard down? My brain kicked fully into gear, and with it so did my wiggly knees, gurgling stomach, and every sweat gland in my body. I turned around.

Josh didn't waste any time smacking the drink out of my hand. Jessica let out a little scream, which Toby laughingly imitated. Panicked, I looked out toward the gym. If I yelled, maybe an adult would hear me, but I saw the doors closing and clicking shut. Through one thin rectangular windowpane, I saw what looked like Mrs. Lutzkraut walking away.

They got me!

And, almost as if reading my mind, Josh said, "No one's saving you this time."

He was right. There was no one around. Jessica, Slim, and Rishi stood frozen. Josh pulled back his right fist and fired.

I tried to jump back, but my fancy wedding shoes had no traction and flew out from underneath me. I let out a shout as I fell backward, feeling one of my hard, pointy shoes connect squarely with Josh's chin. His head snapped back and he barreled into a shocked Toby. As I hit the ground, I saw them smash into the table and watched the punch bowl land on top of them. Josh was dazed and Toby was under him, soaked in red punch. The whole fight lasted about one second.

Slim and Jessica grabbed me by the arms and helped me up. We hurried back into the gym as some of the parents went running over to investigate the loud crash. We could just hear their angry yells before we slipped into the crowd.

Too shaken to dance, we moved to the far corner to catch our breath. Rishi was the first to speak. "All this time, Rodney, you never told us you knew karate!"

"Well, I, uh," I mumbled.

Slim interjected, "Yeah, you yelled just like Bruce Lee as you kicked him!" Slim then yelled a high-pitched karate scream. *"Whaaaaaaaaaaaach oooooooaaaaaaaahhhhh!!"*

"Quiet down, guys," Jessica said, "Rodney might get into big trouble." She was still holding my arm.

At that moment we noticed a pink-stained pair being led out of the gym by a couple of parents and Mr. Feebletop. Both boys looked miserable. Josh stumbled along holding his chin and Toby was limping. Rishi and Slim ran off to tell Dave and Kayla what had just happened.

Jessica remained by my side. "Rodney, I never knew someone could be so brave. Josh is so big and scary. I couldn't move, and you just handled it like it was nothing. You kicked him in the head. *It was like a movie!* You know, you're not only brave, but you're nice, funny, and kind."

"You forgot cute," I joked.

"You *are* cute," she said, smiling. At that very moment

the DJ dimmed the lights and started playing a slower song. I looked over and noticed Rishi at the DJ's side. He gave me the thumbs-up sign. As Jessica and I began to dance, I somehow knew we were going to kiss. I closed my eyes, puckered up, and leaned in.

Her lips felt cold, saggy, and bony, not at all what I had dreamed about for months. I snapped open my eyes and realized I was kissing the back of Mrs. Lutzkraut's hand. "We'll have none of that at this dance! Jessica, go tell Kayla I want her to stop twirling Dave around the room." Jessica and I stood still, gazing at each other. "Run along now, Jessica." She looked disappointed, but headed off into the crowd. As for Mrs. Lutzkraut, she glared at me long and hard before opening her mouth.

"You were in the lobby and caused the whole commotion. I'll make sure that Mr. Feebletop punishes you this time for starting the fight. . . ."

"Oh really?" I asked. "If you saw me there, how come you didn't do anything to stop the fight? In fact, how come you closed the gym doors? And how come you didn't join the parents when they went running in? I'm sure Mr. Feebletop will have a lot of questions for you."

"Why you impudent, ill-mannered . . ." Her head began to shake back and forth as she searched for the right word. She was ready to blow. Finally, still shaking and twitching, she turned and hurried off just as my dad arrived to pick me up.

"Was that Mrs. Lunchbox?" he asked.

"Lutzkraut." I smiled.

"Well she looks kind of batty, if you ask me. Anyway, how was the dance?"

"Great," I answered, taking one last look at Jessica across the gym. "Definitely an evening to remember."

Chapter 27

THE FINAL STRETCH

It was finally here. The last week of school. We were heading to Super Adventure on Tuesday and graduating on Wednesday. Three days left. Sitting in class Monday morning, it seemed like everything was going my way. Mrs. Lutzkraut was running out of time to torture me, news of my ninjalike kick had spread throughout school, and Josh had been missing in action since the dance. I smiled, realizing I might not see him again this year. His partner in crime sat next to me, sulking, but he didn't matter to me anymore. *Time to coast to the finish*, I thought. You'd think I would have learned.

Things didn't start being bad right away. In fact, Monday was pretty normal—if you consider a crazy teacher normal.

"As you know, we are heading to Super Adventure tomorrow," Mrs. Lutzkraut announced. We cheered and immediately her right eyebrow started dancing all around. The thought of us having fun was enough to send her over the edge. "Silence!" she shouted. "I can still cancel tomorrow's excursion if I choose." That shut us up. Satisfied, she continued. "Toby, Mr. Feebletop has informed me that you'll be staying with him tomorrow because of your involvement in a certain incident at the dance. . . ."

"But you said you'd take care of old Feeb. . . ."

"Don't interrupt me, young man!" Mrs. Lutzkraut shouted, suddenly moving toward him like a leopard about to pounce. "A memory can be a *dangerous* thing." Normally that would be an odd comment for a teacher to make, but this was Mrs. Lutzkraut, after all. Toby slunk down into his chair as she stood over him. It was interesting to watch someone else go through a Lutzkraut intimidation session. After a nasty pause she headed to her desk.

Toby wasn't a legendary school thug for nothing, though. As soon as Mrs. Lutzkraut's back was turned, he scrunched up his face and stuck out his tongue.

"It'll be hard to eat lunch without that thing!" she snapped, her back still facing him. The woman definitely had superpowers. Soon enough, I would be using all *my* powers to outsmart her.

The rest of the day I spent as much time as I could with Jessica. We talked about the trip and the summer before us. The late June air was hot, and I soaked it in, feeling good and happy right down to my bones.

That night I was too excited to sleep, but I must have, because the next thing I knew my father was waking me up and it was morning already. A beautiful, sunny morning.

"Rodney, it's five thirty. Time for Super Land."

"Super Adventure," I muttered, getting out of bed.

My class was set to leave an hour before everyone else arrived at school. After a quick breakfast, my dad drove me to Baber and dropped me off in front of the waiting bus. I climbed in and sat down by Rishi, noticing a few chaperones toward the back. Once we got going, Mrs. Lutzkraut stood up, glared at us, and spoke the words I had been sweating.

"I have made up our chaperone groups." I wanted to be with my buddies, but more than that, I desperately hoped Jessica would be with me. Mrs. Lutzkraut rattled off some names. So far, so good. Finally she announced, "As for our last group, the following students will be together: Rodney, Rishi, Tim, Dave, Greg, Kayla, Samantha, and Jessica."

It couldn't have worked out better! It was almost *too* good. Jessica looked over at me, smiling. Rishi shouted, "It's a dream come true!" as he high-fived me.

"Enough of that," Mrs. Lutzkraut interrupted. "Yes, since the eight of you have been so poorly behaved, I have placed you together. And I'll have no problem keeping an eye on you, since *I'll* be your chaperone."

"Dream come true?" I whispered softly to Rishi.

"*Nightmare* is more like it." I pondered a day of Mrs. Lutzkraut. I'd be with seven friends, so I doubted she would try anything fishy, but I also knew she wouldn't allow any fun.

After thirty minutes of driving on the highway past cornfields and truck stops and more cornfields, Mrs. Lutzkraut stood up again and yelled over the noisy bus engine, "May I have your attention?" A couple of the mothers in the back of the bus continued gossiping together. They didn't see the famous Lutzkraut sneer, nor did they see her trudge down the aisle toward them. Again, more nastily, she shouted, "I would appreciate your attention!" The chaperones snapped to. They looked at her looming over them and shriveled a bit. Mrs. Lutzkraut's wilting stare lingered on the two moms for a few seconds more before she turned back and faced the rest of us.

"I want to go over our day," she began. "Each chaperone group may go where they want."

"We want to go on roller coasters!" Rishi blurted.

"And visit the snack stands," Slim added.

Mrs. Lutzkraut's glare became as hard as marble. She continued more slowly in a clipped, annoyed tone that no one dared interrupt.

"Rishi, maybe you'd like to enjoy the inside of this bus today. And, chaperones," she added, turning to the two moms in the back, "you must focus on your students. This is not a vacation for you." They shrank even farther down in the green seats. "Do not get separated from your group." Then she turned from the moms and had a special message just for me. "Remember, Rodney, amusement parks can be dangerous places."

Chapter 28

SUPER ADVENTURE

Mrs. Lutzkraut's warning, "Amusement parks can be dangerous places," still echoed in my head as we pulled up at Super Adventure. What had she meant by that? I watched her get off the bus and walk through the parking lot. I assumed she was going to buy the tickets, but then she cut through two rows of cars and stopped by a . . . no, it couldn't be. It was the red car.

I elbowed Rishi. "Hey, who is she talking to over there?"

"Who?"

"Mrs. Lutzkraut."

"Who cares? Can you see it? There, in the distance, it's Destination Death, the highest, fastest, most deadly roller coaster in America. It's calling us. Do you hear it? 'Rahhhhdney, Rahhhhdney, come ride me,'" he chanted in my ear. "I know you hear it. That thing will scare the pants right off ya."

Watching Mrs. Lutzkraut was what was scaring the pants off me. She was leaning over that car talking to some woman wearing a big scarf and sunglasses. Every once in a while she would point back toward us. Eventually the woman got out and the two of them approached the bus. Only Mrs. Lutzkraut climbed back in.

"Rodney, can you join me for a second?" She headed back into the parking lot.

My heart was pounding. Everyone was staring at me. "What'd you do, Rodney?" Rishi asked.

"Nothing," I muttered, "but I think I'm about to get kidnapped."

The perfect day I had planned with Jessica and my friends was going horribly wrong. I walked down the bus steps and faced the woman. Behind the scarf and sunglasses there was something familiar about her. I had seen that nose before. It was long and pointy. . . . Of course! Long Nose. I began to shake, remembering how crazy she had acted that day with the basketball.

"I see you recognize Ms. Whiner," Lutzkraut piped up.

"Uh," I choked.

"Yes, well, since you've behaved so badly this year, I knew I needed a little extra help with you today. Ms. Whiner will personally watch your every move."

"I'm not sure Mr. Feebletop . . ." I began.

"Don't mention his name, you little brat," Long Nose

finally spoke, rubbing the back of her head. "After what you did to me with that basketball, you'd better just concentrate on getting through today."

Mrs. Lutzkraut turned to me. "Mr. Feebletop will learn that I took every precaution to keep my students safe. After all, Rodney, your *safety* is my greatest concern." I shivered at that, but was glad when she finally asked everyone to exit the bus. The class immediately noticed Long Nose, who stood a few paces away.

"Hey, didn't she get fired?" Rishi asked.

Long Nose evidently heard the comment. "I am a chaperone for this trip, and as such, I don't need to be an employee. Plus, I have the power to exclude you from any ride or activity."

Rishi, not wanting to foil his trip to Destination Death, just said, "Well, it's nice to see you again." Long Nose didn't answer. The feeling wasn't mutual.

It was early in the day but Super Adventure was already very much alive. I could hear the rumble of roller coasters streaking down from peaks. Screams filled the air. What I heard, Slim smelled. His nostrils were twitching, and I could see his taste buds taking it all in. Super Adventure had something for everyone. For me, that "something" was the blond-haired girl walking next to me.

We were having fun pointing things out. "Look, Rodney, do you see the photo booth?" Jessica asked. "Let's get our picture taken." We parted from the slow-moving class and climbed into the little booth and pulled back the curtain. My mind wasn't on the picture. Maybe this was it. I slid the money into the bill collector and looked at Jessica, her eyes were twinkling in the dark. *Okay, Rathbone*, I told myself. Time to make my . . .

"Aha! Trying to escape!" Long Nose stuck her head in, foiling my kiss attempt as the camera flashed. Just as she tried to open her eyes, the second flash struck. Temporarily blinded and screaming, she ripped the curtain from the booth and stumbled away from the two of us. We had time for one brief smile before the fourth and last picture clicked and we followed her out.

Long Nose was ranting to herself as Mrs. Lutzkraut approached Jessica and me. "You two are not to be alone together again. In fact, Rodney, I want you to hold Ms. Whiner's hand." Neither of us liked that idea. Long Nose took out some antibacterial gel and squirted my hand before grabbing it.

She had dragged me around before, and my mouth blurted, "Just like old times."

"I have to hold your filthy hand, but I will not listen to your filthy mouth all day. No talking." This was shaping up to be the worst day any kid could ever have at an amusement park. I knew we needed to get away from our jailors, but the hand held me tight. Escape wouldn't be easy.

"Are you ready for some rides?" Mrs. Lutzkraut asked.

"Absolutely!" Rishi yelled.

"That's good," she answered, looking at me and not at Rishi. "Why don't we head to my *favorite* ride?"

"Destination Death?" Rishi inquired.

"No, we won't be going anywhere near that one today."

Rishi looked crestfallen. As we meandered through the crowds, I pondered what ride could possibly be Mrs. Lutzkraut's favorite. As it turned out, I was pleasantly surprised. We arrived in front of the bumper cars. The line was short, and it wasn't long before I was rushing out searching for the perfect car.

I climbed in, put the one strap over my shoulder, and pressed down several times on the accelerator waiting for the car to zoom to life. I glanced around. When I felt the car hum, I already had my first victim in my sights. Kayla was too busy eyeing Dave to notice me swooping in from behind. I had built up a fair amount of speed and was closing in when I was met by a jarring crash. My head snapped back and I turned to see Mrs. Lutzkraut laughing behind me in a black bumper car painted with red and orange flames.

She laughed harder still as another car, driven by Long Nose, swept in and crunched me from the right. I was tossed around the car like a rag doll. Mrs. Lutzkraut smashed me again from behind, and now I hit the pedal trying to escape. I zoomed off away from them, with Long Nose hot on my tail. I tried some fancy maneuvers in an effort to lose her, but I couldn't shake her. Finally,

I faked a left but pulled hard to the right around Dave, who was trying to escape from Kayla. I was met head on by Mrs. Lutzkraut. Seconds later Long Nose collided with me from behind. I found myself sandwiched between a pair of cackling witches.

The cars finally died and I breathed a sigh of relief. Leaving the ride, Mrs. Lutzkraut and Long Nose could barely walk, but not because they were in pain. The two of them were now laughing so hard that Mrs. Lutzkraut had to bend over and hold her side. "Ima," she was trying to tell Long Nose, "I don't think I've ever had so much fun."

"We hit that Rathbone kid so hard that my kerchief flew off!" That started the two of them laughing again and I realized this was my chance.

"Rishi," I whispered. "Time to make our escape. Spread the word." I waited until he had whispered to everyone in our group before shouting, "Run!"

If you were there, you would have seen eight kids tearing through the park, bumping into people and jumping over garbage cans, but you wouldn't have seen any adults, because after a few hundred yards Mrs. Lutzkraut and Long Nose were nowhere to be seen.

We all laughed and slowly settled down. Samantha, however, was worried that we were now in big trouble.

"It'll be okay, Sam," Jessica told her. "It's the second to last day of school. What can they really do to us?"

"Besides," Rishi added, "they'll be sure to blame Rodney and not you."

With those wonderful words of encouragement, Samantha relaxed. "Hey, did you hear Lutzkraut call Long Nose something like Ima?" she asked.

"Yeah, I guess that's her name," I answered.

After a minute it was Jessica who asked, "Wait, her name is Ima Whiner?"

All eight of us burst out laughing and shouted her full name to everyone we passed. People just looked at us and shook their heads.

"All right, enough goofin' around," Rishi announced. "Now that we ditched those two, time for Destination Death!"

My good mood vanished. I wanted no part of it and began fishing for an excuse. Fortunately, Jessica grabbed my arm and opened her mouth to offer an excuse of her own. "Why don't we check out *that* ride?"

We all turned to where she was looking. There, right in front of us, was the Tunnel of Love. I wondered if she was thinking what I was thinking.

Samantha giggled but Rishi looked annoyed. "That ride's a joke. Let's go hit the coasters."

"I don't know, it sounds like a good ride to me," Kayla chimed in. I noticed her looking at Dave. This was my chance.

"Guys, it's a log flume," I pointed out. "Look at the sign." Indeed the sign showed a boat pouring through a heart and down a big waterfall. "That's a serious drop." Eventually, everyone agreed to go on the ride. Rishi liked the idea of traveling down a waterfall, Slim was busy eating hot dogs and didn't care where we went, Kayla was eyeing Dave, and Samantha was giggling, pinching Greg. Finally, Jessica and I would be alone.

The four-minute ride had an hour line. Rishi was getting itchy by the time we neared the end, and when we read that the waterfall was temporarily closed, he almost went nuts. Evidently there were two ways for the heart-shaped boats to exit the tunnel—the crashing waterfall or the slow-traveling river, which was still operating. Rishi may have been furious, but all I cared about was Jessica, and to be honest, the slower the better.

The first boat pulled up. Kayla grabbed Dave and shoved him aboard, and I wondered if that's how British sailors were shanghaied into the navy years ago. Samantha giggled and nodded at Greg, who joined her. Jessica and I waited for the next boat. Rishi said, "Have a niiiice time, you two."

"You two have a nice time too," I replied. It hadn't dawned on Rishi and Slim that they'd be together in the Tunnel of Love. They looked at each other. "Aghhhhhhh."

It was then that we heard the shout. "There they are!" Long Nose and Mrs. Lutzkraut had shown up just as Jessica and I climbed into our boat and floated off on our voyage. Mrs. Lutzkraut frantically tried to push her way through the crowds. "No boys and girls together!

Rodney, you're in big trouble! Climb out of that heart thing!" she screamed.

I waved and shouted back, "Wish me a bon voyage!" With that, we rounded the corner. I looked at Jessica. She smiled, slightly nervous. I felt more confident. I leaned in, put my arm around her shoulder, and said, "Now, where were we?"

She giggled and leaned closer.

"That's what I thought," I answered, and went to make my move.

"Rodney Rathbone! Remove your hands from that girl." I jumped and spun around. About twenty feet back, in the next boat, stood Mrs. Lutzkraut, and she wasn't alone. Also trying to stand, but holding on for dear life, was Long Nose. They must have taken Slim and Rishi's boat.

Jessica sighed. "Rodney, we'll find time later, maybe." I realized yet another chance to kiss her was foiled, but I had greater concerns—namely, my life. We were in a bad spot alone in the tunnel. I looked back again and saw Lutzkraut and Long Nose pushing furiously against the tunnel walls, moving their boat forward.

They were gaining ground. I gulped. What would they do to me? Would they board our boat like some savage pirates?

"Rodney, they're after us," Jessica added. Something about the tone in her voice made me take control—and for once not act like a coward!

I'd put up with enough and I wasn't going down without a fight. It was time I did something for myself and, shockingly, I did. We were more than halfway down the river now and I could see a fork up ahead. There was a bumper that forced our boat to the right onto Romance River. The other way splashed along to the now-closed Wicked Waterfall. I saw the signs and then I saw something else as our boat started to head down the river. Back behind a dancing cupid was a large red button. Below the button was a sign that read MAIN BUMPER SWITCH. I realized that the button controlled the bumper that pushed the boats either onto the river or waterfall.

"Hold me!" I shouted to Jessica.

"Don't you dare touch him," yelled Lutzkraut from behind.

I looked Jessica in the eyes and whispered, "Hold me so I don't fall." I jumped up and leaned all the way over as Jessica grabbed my waist. As we passed the button I was just able to reach it with one finger, but that was enough. I felt it click and glanced back. The bumper that was blocking the waterfall shifted and blocked the river as Mrs. Lutzkraut and Long Nose reached the fork. Slowly their confident, evil looks changed to surprise and panic as they headed away from us down another tube of water. Mrs. Lutzkraut yelled, "What's this? Not the waterfall! Turn off the ride! Turn off the ride! Noooo!!!!!!!" and off they floated.

Jessica sat looking at me with a mixture of surprise

and excitement. "You're unbelievable. We're probably going to get arrested."

"If that's true, we might as well enjoy our last moments of freedom."

And we did.

Before long, our boat floated out into the light of day—in time for us to see Slim and Rishi barreling down the Wicked Waterfall. They screamed the whole way and I knew Rishi loved it. The same couldn't be said for the park employees, who were running around trying to figure out why heart-shaped boats were shooting out of the "closed" waterfall.

Mrs. Lutzkraut's boat bumped to a stop in the unloading area. She was drenched and shoving Long Nose to climb out. I guess Long Nose wasn't moving fast enough because Lutzkraut gave her such a hard second shove that she toppled into the canal. Long Nose stood up in a foot of water, screaming.

Lutzkraut was proving to be every bit as crazy as I knew her to be. Her hair was matted and stuck to her head. Her dress was dripping, and dark mascara ran down her cheeks. A Super Adventure attendant came over to help her off the boat. Lutzkraut swung her pocketbook at him and screamed, "Your rides are faulty! This place should be shut down!"

We didn't stick around to hear the rest. I breathed in the amusement park air and strolled leisurely through the park with Jessica at my side. Eventually Rishi and the gang got to ride Destination Death while Jessica and I ordered lunch. By all accounts the coaster was scary, but not as much fun as the Tunnel of Love.

As we headed back to the bus I was careful to let go of Jessica's hand before we ran into Mrs. Lutzkraut, who stood before the bus holding a clipboard. She was busy counting students and chaperones. While dried, her hair was still messy. Makeup ran down from her eyes, and she looked even scarier than normal. Her dress was wrinkly and disheveled.

"Did you have a nice time today?" I asked. "It was wonderful seeing Ms. Whiner. I sure am going to miss you two."

For a brief moment I thought she was going to hit me over the head with the clipboard. I saw her fingers changing color as they gripped it tighter. Through clenched teeth and a manic twitch, she was barely able to get out the words "Sit down."

I did, right next to Jessica. Most of the way back we laughed and talked about the day at Super Adventure. We also spoke about the school year that was quickly coming to a close.

"Hey Rodney," she said at one point. "You really lucked out. I just realized that you made it through the whole year without having to face your worst fear."

I wasn't sure which of my many fears she was talking about. "Uh, yeah," I started to answer, not knowing what to say.

"I mean, you didn't have to stand up in class and do a book report and you didn't even have to make a speech when we did *Robin Hood*. It's so funny that someone like you hates public speaking, but don't worry, your secret's safe with me."

Out of habit I turned around to make sure no one was listening—and almost jumped. Mrs. Lutzkraut was leaning forward in the seat right behind us. That sneak was trying to listen to our conversation. She looked into my eyes and I realized I had never been so close to her face. It was truly horrifying. For a second neither of us moved. Then, slowly, without removing her gaze from mine, she leaned back and lifted her chin slightly. A wicked smile played around her lips.

I turned around and whispered to Jessica, "Let's change the subject."

For the rest of the ride back we made sure to keep our voices down. I couldn't be sure whether Lutzkraut had overheard our conversation. By the time we got off the bus, though, it was the last thing on my mind. I saw my father waiting to pick me up and, as I said good-bye to my friends, I realized I had just enjoyed the best day of my life. Super Adventure had definitely lived up to its name—and all I had left of the school year was tomorrow's graduation.

"How were the rides?" my dad asked as we drove off.

"Fine," I said.

"I bet none of them were as good as the Cyclone."

"I don't know about that, Dad. I'm pretty sure one of them was actually better."

We both smiled for different reasons. At the time, neither of us could have imagined the terrifying ups and downs that awaited me the following day.

Chapter 29

GRADUATION DAY

"Oh, aren't you just the dashing graduate," my great-aunt Evelyn greeted me the next morning. I didn't know she was coming, but I was never shocked to see her.

"Thanks for coming, Aunt Evelyn."

"Well I couldn't miss my nephew's big day. I was vacationing with Victor in Prague, but I was able to fly in late last night."

Victor Johnson? I wondered.

I had slept late that morning and was rushing around to get dressed for graduation. I was excited about the last day of school and was equally looking forward to seeing Jessica after the Tunnel of Love and the bus ride home. I knew, now, that it was time to ask her out for real, and for the first time all year, I was sure she'd say yes.

The family piled into the car and drove me to school. I was dropped off at the front and my parents, aunt, and

Penny went into the gym to reserve the best seats.

Pretty soon I joined the rest of the class and noticed how dressed up everyone was. Slim was actually wearing a tuxedo. "Hey 007, you all set for graduation?" I asked. He just gave me a look that told me he was miserable. The tuxedo might have fit him the last time he wore it, but now it was so tight around his stomach that two buttons had actually popped off.

Why do moms put their sons through the agony of dressy clothes? I wondered.

All the girls wore dresses and had corsages wrapped around their wrists. We didn't have caps and gowns, since Mrs. Lutzkraut had said they were only for high school kids. According to her, we were just finishing our time at Baber and moving up to middle school and therefore, not truly graduating. That woman sure knew how to spoil every occasion—which I was about to be reminded of one last time.

Not counting Mrs. Lutzkraut, everyone was excited, and Rishi looked ready to burst. "Hey Rodney, I have a little surprise cooked up today." I looked at his twinkling eyes and thought: *Here we go again*.

"Rishi, don't do anything crazy. I just want to enjoy the moment. . . ."

"Don't worry, you're going to love it. Probably more than anyone. Besides, it's too late for me to change anything now." There was nothing I could do, so hopefully I really would like his surprise. Besides, what trouble could he possibly cook up on the last day?

Before long, we were walking down to the gym where the ceremony was taking place. Ms. Dearing's class was already filing in and I could hear Mrs. Panic playing "Pomp and Circumstance" on the piano. Just as our class was getting ready to sit in our seats on the stage, I noticed Mrs. Lutzkraut. She still had that strange smile on her face. I'd been down this road too many times before and knew bad news was coming before she opened her mouth. She motioned me aside.

"After your actions yesterday, I went straight to Mr. Feebletop. I wouldn't be one bit surprised if he held back your diploma."

Could he do that? *Would* he do that? I tried not to worry and took a seat after Kayla. We were sitting alphabetically, and I was happy that Rishi's last name was Singh and just after mine.

He sat down and laughed. "Did you see Josh? I think his chin is wired shut. He looks ridiculous. Oh man, I can't wait for my surprise."

As we said the pledge and sang "My Country, 'Tis of Thee," I looked out at all the parents and teachers. Occasionally flashes from cameras flickered in the audience. Finally, Mr. Feebletop took the podium. "Congratulations to our graduates. We will now begin to call students up to receive their diplomas. I will call each student alphabetically, and I assure you, we will pause long enough for a nice picture." I saw Dave's dad inching down the aisle, camera ready. "Okay, we will begin with David Anderson." Dave was met by applause and some cheers, the loudest coming from Kayla on my right.

"Rodney, doesn't he look good in a tie?"

"Uh, I guess." I wasn't really paying attention to Kayla, or even the large crowd of family members sitting in the audience looking up at us. I was watching Mrs. Lutzkraut standing next to Mr. Feebeltop. She saw me and gave me a little wave. I looked away from her and continued quietly watching other students receive their diplomas.

"Kayla Radisson," Mr. Feebletop called out. She got up and walked to the podium wearing a big smile. This was it. I was next. Mr. Feebletop cleared his throat and coughed for a brief second, and then said, "This morning I was met by the next graduate's teacher. She implored me not to hand out his diploma with everyone else's. She mentioned that it wasn't what he deserved, and I realized she was right. You see, some students continually do things that separate them from the group, and they don't deserve to be treated the same as everyone else. Yes, some students do so much *more* that they deserve special recognition."

A smile spread across my face and I let out a sigh of relief. The same couldn't be said of Mrs. Lutzkraut. She looked horrified as Mr. Feebletop continued. "Yes, this year I've been astounded by one young man who has impressed me more than any student I can remember, so

I wholeheartedly agree with his teacher that he deserves a little extra recognition."

"No!" Mrs. Lutzkraut screeched.

Mr. Feebletop laughed. "No? I realize, Mrs. Lutzkraut, that you want to make this a special moment, but I think he should receive his diploma now. Let us formally invite our Star Student of the Year up here."

"But, but, but . . ." Mrs. Lutzkraut looked like she was on the verge of collapse. Mr. Feebletop reached back and patted her shoulder.

"I know it's very hard to say good-bye to one of your favorites, Mrs. Lutzkraut, but all good things must come to an end. Rodney Rathbone, come on up here. . . ."

The crowd roared as I walked to Mr. Feebletop. He reached out and shook my hand. After the clapping died down he continued. "Mrs. Lutzkraut, you may do the honors." He handed her my diploma. She just stood there, face twitching.

"Mrs. Lutzkraut? Rodney's diploma?" She looked like she had eaten something rotten. Mr. Feebletop turned back to the microphone. "She's overcome by emotion. It's okay, Mrs. Lutzkraut. Let me help you." Grudgingly, with some assistance from Mr. Feebletop, she held out her hand.

I couldn't resist one last jab. I said loudly, "I'm going to miss you, too," and reached out and hugged her. I could feel her squirm as the audience let out one big sentimental, "AAAAAwwwwwwwwwwww!!!"

Mr. Feebletop nodded his head as if to say, *See? It's stuff like this that makes him special.*

Mrs. Lutzkraut looked like she was going to be sick but managed to hold it together. Then, strangely, her eyes began to twinkle and that devilish smile from yesterday returned to her face. I gulped. My whole life with her had become one enormous chess match and she was about to make her next move. I was in trouble.

She turned from me and joined Mr. Feebletop at the microphone. "He certainly is a unique child, Mr. Feebletop. May I make a suggestion?" My pulse quickened.

The crowd perked up, wondering what was going on. I eyed the exit door as she cleared her throat and continued. "I think it would be just terrific if Rodney made a little speech to say farewell to the school that loves him so dearly. After all, it's not every day we have an opportunity to hear from such a fine young man."

What? She'd got me! She had overheard Jessica on the bus and knew about my fear of public speaking. I looked out at the hundreds of faces, began to get dizzy, and realized that Mrs. Lutzkraut had won the match.

"Well, I'm not sure," Mr. Feebletop observed. "After all, he's unprepared and . . ."

"Oh, I'm sure *his* mouth can handle it." Mrs. Lutzkraut smiled.

"Well, hmmm . . . Rodney, what do you say?"

Before I could answer, Rishi started shouting, "Speech!

Speech! Speech!" The entire gymnasium joined him.

Mrs. Lutzkraut began to fist-pump in time to the "speech" chant. Then she turned to me and I felt her bony fingers guide me to the microphone. My chest was pounding so hard that I wondered if it was possible for a kid my age to have a heart attack. My breaths were short and panicked. I felt my peripheral vision narrowing, and I prayed I wouldn't collapse right off the stage.

My mind, as usual, began to search for the perfect excuse to get me out of this—and then it struck me. For the first time in my life I realized there was another option. Instead of taking the coward's way out, I could actually face my fear. Maybe I didn't have to rely on blind luck to save me. It felt so strange to think this way, like I had someone else's brain in my head.

Mrs. Lutzkraut thrust the microphone into my hand. "We're all waiting," she announced. Then, under her breath she added, "I'm going to enjoy this."

I looked over at my friends yelling "Speech" and couldn't believe my train of thought. I was really considering going through with it. It was now or never. For better or for worse, I decided to make the speech.

"Good morning," I tried to say, but nothing came out. The crowd was looking up expectantly and I felt my face turn red hot. I had to calm down. I remembered something I had seen on TV, that if you're nervous about speaking in front of people you should picture them in their underwear.

I had nothing to lose. I looked out and a smile spread across my face. Maybe this would actually work. Seeing people without their clothes on was funny and oddly relaxing.

I took a deep breath and was just bringing the microphone to my mouth when I caught sight of Mrs. Lutzkraut. Before I could stop it, an image far too disturbing for a boy my age sprang to mind. "Uuuuuuuughhhhh!" I cringed.

"We can't hear you!" someone yelled from the back of the audience.

Keep it together, I told myself. It was then that the new, grown-up–sounding voice inside my head made a suggestion. *Rodney, why not just tell them the truth?*

I cleared my throat and heard it echo off the walls. "The truth is," I began, "I'm not a great public speaker. I've always been scared of it. . . ."

"Yeah right!" Rishi yelled. The auditorium laughed.

I looked out at everyone and went on. "Many of you know that this was my first year at Baber. I remember the first day. I was really nervous about coming here that day. . . ."

"Good one, Rodney!" Slim shouted. "I guess you knocked out Josh to calm your nerves!" Laughs filled the air. I noticed Josh sink lower in his seat.

Again, I started up, and this time it was a bit easier. "I want to thank everyone here: my parents, Mr. Feebletop. . . ."

"Don't forget Jessica!" Kayla hollered. More laughs and my cheeks felt hot again, this time for a different reason.

I was starting to feel good. I could handle speaking up here. Maybe it wasn't the Gettysburg Address, but I didn't care. I was facing a fear, and for me, the moment was special.

I looked at the crowd. My friends were smiling and laughing, as were most of the students. I realized that all of them had changed during the year. The look of fear was gone from their faces, and it made me feel good. I continued. "This year, I learned a lot, but I think the most important lesson I learned is that even a new kid can fit right in if he's lucky enough to make good friends."

"You know it!" Dave yelled. Even quiet Dave was getting in on the action. The peanut gallery was in rare form and I realized there wasn't much point in continuing.

"Before I turn the microphone back to Mr. Feebletop, I want to end by thanking Mrs. Lutzkraut for this nice opportunity to say a few words." I paused and smiled in her direction. "Finally, have a great summer, everyone; see you in Garretsville Middle School; and let's go, Mets!"

I looked out at the cheering crowd. At times, being the hero puts you in a tight spot, but the rewards can be pretty darn good. As if emphasizing my thought, Jessica blew me a kiss.

I was feeling such a high of relief and happiness that I almost floated back to my seat. As I moseyed past Mrs. Lutzkraut, I smiled and asked under my breath, "Got any more surprises for me?"

Through clenched teeth she answered, "You bet I do, Rathbone. By this time tomorrow you'll know which one of us has won."

I sat down, wondering for a moment what she meant, but I shrugged it off. After all, the school year was over in about twenty minutes. What could she possibly do to me now?

Chapter 30

AND THE WINNER IS . . .

Once the commotion had died down and the rest of the diplomas had been handed out, Mr. Feebletop announced that it was time to watch a video recap of the year. We moved to several empty rows reserved for us in the audience. With Louis Armstrong singing "What a Wonderful World," the slide show began of our past year at Baber.

"Get ready," Rishi whispered.

Everything started fine. There were pictures of all us kids, including ones of me. In one slide I was being cheered at field day. Someone burst into applause and I turned around just in time to see my mom elbowing my dad, who abruptly stopped clapping. In another shot, some of us were sitting together at our Halloween party in Mrs. Lutzkraut's class. Nothing seemed out of the ordinary. Rishi, however, was rocking back and forth in anticipation. All of a sudden a picture of Toby picking his nose popped up. There was a roar from the audience, and I noticed the computer ladies look at each other. Toby's mouth fell open and his cheeks got dark red. Rishi said, "Wait, it gets better."

Another roar of laughter brought my attention back to the screen. This time it wasn't Toby. It was Josh. There he was, spread out in the grass with a bloody nose on the first day of school. I laughed along with everyone else, but that familiar feeling of dread began to creep up my spine. The next picture flashed up. This one had Josh again, only now he was on the bus with a swollen black-and-blue nose. I bit my lip, knowing this wasn't good. Meanwhile, Rishi elbowed me and howled with laughter. *You idiot*, I thought. *Can't you just leave well enough alone?* I noticed the computer ladies poking around trying to figure out what was going on.

Flash! Josh afraid of the skull outside Old Man Johnson's.

Flash! Josh standing in the snow with a big rip in his leather jacket.

Flash! Josh covered in pink punch holding his chin.

Come on, computer ladies. Pull the plug. Rishi was doubled over, helpless with laughter, tears running down his face. I looked back in the crowd trying to see Josh, but couldn't find him.

Flash! Josh covered in mud on field day . . .

"Stop it!!!" Josh exploded. You couldn't miss him now. Screaming at the top of his lungs, he ran to the front and jumped up, trying to pull the screen down. He couldn't reach it and was yelling and ranting crazily like a dog trying to attack a cat up in a tree. After jumping seven or eight times, he gave up his attempts, deciding instead to pull the plug from the wall with a jerk.

By this time Mr. Borus and Mr. Ball arrived and guided a flailing Josh out of the gym.

Just as he was pushing through the door, he uttered a final yell. "You think this is funny, Rathbone? I'll get you for this!" The threat echoed through the stunned crowd.

"That was awesome." Rishi laughed. "I knew he'd go berserk."

Yeah, real awesome, I thought. *What could be better than getting your enemy even madder?*

Mr. Feebletop walked up to the podium. "My deepest apologies. In all my years as a principal I have never had such a moment in my building. I'm embarrassed and I'm sorry. Nevertheless, the game must go on . . . I mean, this remains a special day, and while I think we may have had enough pictures for now, there is always time for cake and refreshments. So, please begin heading down to the cafeteria. Thank you." Then he turned to me. "Rodney, meet me in my office. I'll be there in just a minute."

"All right, Mr. Feebletop," I answered, just as my parents, sister, and aunt reached me.

I assured the family that everything was fine and headed down to the office, not knowing what to expect.

I was sitting there looking up at Tom Seaver when Mr. Feebletop walked in. I was slightly nervous. If he thought I was behind that fiasco, it might be too big a problem for him to overlook.

"What a morning, Rodney. Your friend Rishi stopped me in the hall and explained that you had nothing to do with the slides. . . ."

"Is he in trouble?" I asked.

"Not too much. It's the last day of school. And besides, he was smart enough to leave me out of any embarrassing pictures. Anyway, Rodney, what did you want to see me about?"

Before I could explain that *he* had asked to see me, a secretary interrupted. "Mr. and Mrs. Dumbrowski are here with Josh." Mr. Feebletop put the ball down and motioned to send them in.

Sandwiched between his mom and dad, Josh walked in glaring at me and holding his chin. I wasn't too concerned, since I'd soon be away from him for the summer. Mr. Feebletop launched right into it.

"Mr. and Mrs. Dumbrowski, I apologize that your son was singled out in the slide show, but that was a most disrespectful performance put on by Josh today. And it was just last week that he destroyed our punch table with his chin."

Josh's mom started to cry and his dad said, "I don't know what else to do with him. We've tried every solution we can think of."

"How about military school?" I suggested. It just came out. Mr. Feebletop gave me a quick, stern look, but then seemed to ponder what I had said. Josh's parents stared at me, then at each other, then at their son, then back at me.

"That is an excellent idea!" Josh's dad finally exclaimed. "What is your name again, son?"

"Rodney."

Mr. Feebletop explained proudly, "You can see why we gave him extra attention at today's ceremony. He's always thinking. Anyway, I have some brochures here in my filing cabinet. The discipline at Brokenchild Academy is second to none."

"Discipline is exactly what my son needs," Josh's dad said. "That sounds like the perfect school for him. Give me the number. We'll send him there as soon as he gets home from summer camp—the one Mrs. Lutzkraut recommended for him. Camp Wy-Mee."

Then, for the first time, Mr. Feebletop seemed to realize that I didn't belong there. "Oh Rodney, you don't have to stay. Go, enjoy some cake."

"Okay then," I answered, rising to leave. "Well, glad I could help. And Josh, enjoy your new school. Send me a postcard."

Josh was seething, but his mom said, "What a nice boy."

When I arrived in the cafeteria, I explained to my parents and friends that I wasn't in trouble. When I told Rishi about Josh he joked, "You see how brilliant my plans are? I got Josh sent to reform school." I felt like telling him that I'd appreciate his brilliance a whole lot more if it didn't always get me in trouble. Instead I saw Jessica beckoning to me from the hall and went right over.

"So, Rodney, summer's finally here."

"It is," I agreed, sliding up to her.

"You going to ask me something?"

I knew it was time to spit out the question. "Jessica, would you be my girlfriend?"

"I will," she replied. "And as boyfriend and girlfriend, we'll be going to the beach, the pool, the park, and the movies. It's going to be the best summer ever."

"Totally agree," I said, and I meant it. Life couldn't get any better, but then she kissed me and it did!

I left Jessica and my friends and rejoined my family and Aunt Evelyn. We walked out to the car and drove off to the Brick Tavern for Freddy Burgers. I watched the town go by through the open car windows and couldn't remember ever being so happy. For the first time in months, I actually relaxed and let my mind drift. I wondered if I had changed. Maybe everything wasn't just blind luck. Maybe some of my reputation *was* deserved. Besides, now with the threat of Josh out of my life, I could forget about my tough guy reputation and finally be myself. I felt like a new person.

We slowed down and stopped at a red light. Penny poked me. "Hey, isn't that your friend?" she teased.

I turned to the right. Josh was sitting in the backseat of his father's car, shaking a fist in my direction. I just smiled back. "No hard feelings, buddy," I called over to him, rubbing my chin. He was about to get shipped off to camp for the whole summer and would soon be a distant, harmless memory. "Be sure to weave me a basket!"

"Well, what do you know?" my mother suddenly pointed out excitedly. "It's Mrs. Lutzkraut and her friend."

I followed her gaze to the left. Alongside us, stopped in the turning lane, was Long Nose's red car. Mrs. Lutzkraut poked her head out of the passenger window and gave us a little wave. "Who won, Rodney?"

I had no idea what she was talking about. "Which game?" my dad asked her.

As their light turned green, Mrs. Lutzkraut shouted back, "Ask Rodney! By now he should know the score." I could see her and Long Nose giggling as they drove off.

My dad shook his head. "I'll say it again. That lady's nuttier than a . . ."

"Now, now," my mother patted his arm. "Don't say anything that will take away from the surprise."

"Surprise?" I asked excitedly.

"Well," my dad began, "your mother and I are so

proud of your accomplishments this year that we thought it'd be nice to give you a special reward." I liked the sound of that. "We already paid for the whole thing, so you don't need to worry about the expense." I liked the sound of that, too. Maybe it was a new bike. "Yes, son. Your mother and I have decided to send you to sleep-away camp this summer."

"What?" I screamed.

"You see," my mom said, turning around to face me, "Mrs. Lutzkraut recommended it and said it would be an excellent surprise. She even suggested one particular camp. It's called Camp Wy-Mee. You leave tomorrow."

"Rodney," my father added with a big grin, "what could be better than going to sleep-away camp for the whole summer?"

I couldn't answer. I was too busy picturing Josh chasing me through the woods.

"Rodney's turning green!" Penny shouted.

Panic flashed across my dad's face. "Oh no. Not again . . ."

SCOTT STARKEY is an elementary school teacher, soccer coach, and father of three. This is his first novel. He lives in Long Island, New York, with his family.